MONSTER

DANI RENÉ

AUTHOR'S NOTE

Dear Reader,

You're about to meet the men of the Belfast chapter of the Royal Bastards MC. I've had such fun writing these characters, and I'm looking forward to bringing you each member's story.

First, we meet Monster, the President of the MC. This isn't a dark story, I would say it's grey-ish. It's gritty and raw. And I hope you fall for these characters just as much as I have.

Please note, this is written in British English, with Irish slang, so some words may be spelled differently than what you're used to. It is a work of fiction, and some details may have been embellished slightly.

Now, dive in and meet the Royal Bastards.

Mad love,

Dani, xo

She is a vision
Ones eyes cannot hide
His passion her envy
Two worlds would collide

Allured by temptation
Hearts burning with fear
Griefs quiet reminder
Attraction grows near

Their hunger so primal
Forbidden this trance
Secrets abundant
An entangled romance

Though questions unanswered
As fate takes desire
Emotions inflamed
Pure love meets with fire

Singed
_hydrus

More from Hydrus at
www.hydruspoetry.com

ROYAL BASTARDS CODE

PROTECT: The club and your brothers come before anything else, and must be protected at all costs. CLUB is FAMILY.

RESPECT: Earn it & Give it. Respect club law. Respect the patch. Respect your brothers. Disrespect a member and there will be hell to pay.

HONOR: Being patched in is an honor, not a right. Your colors are sacred, not to be left alone, and NEVER let them touch the ground.

OL' LADIES: Never disrespect a member's or brother's Ol'Lady. PERIOD.

CHURCH is MANDATORY.

LOYALTY: Takes precedence over all, including well-being.

HONESTY: Never LIE, CHEAT, or STEAL from another member or the club.

TERRITORY: You are to respect your brother's property and follow their Chapter's club rules.

TRUST: Years to earn it...seconds to lose it.

NEVER RIDE OFF: Brothers do not abandon their family.

PLAYLIST

Drive You Insane - Daniel Di Angelo
Dancer in the Dark - For My Pain
Shiver - Echos
Guest Room - Echos
Ride On - Christy Moore
Do You Remember - Jarryd James
Monster - Skillet
Like A Villain - Bad Omens
How to Save a Life - The Fray

Find the full playlist on Spotify

PROLOGUE

Monster

10 years ago

I was brought up a religious Catholic boy. My ma made sure I went to church every Sunday and said my prayers every night. Even though I was convinced talking to a man I couldn't see was stupid, she would slap me about the head and tell me to do it anyway. Her influence on my life is the reason I'm here today, alive and not lying beside my da six feet under. She needed me just as much as I needed her. At twenty-eight, I still live with her, wanting to show her that no matter what, I'll be by her side.

I obeyed the rules she set out for me when I was growin' up. Made sure I didn't get myself into trouble, at least for a while. It wasn't until I hit sixteen and got into life with the motorcycle club that it all went south. Which brings me to today. The whispers I'll be takin' over from Da have been nonstop over the past couple weeks, and I'm pretty sure Ma has been dreading this day since she had me.

The thing is, I tried. I truly did. I wanted to be the son my ma could be proud of, and even though I've done some stupid shite, I still know right from wrong. I watched Da fuck up too many times to count, and I vowed to never be like him.

You can't stay innocent forever. Not when you live in Belfast. Northern Ireland has always been famous for the shite that goes down on the daily. It's as if the world is watching, waiting for another storm to hit. Violence was a way of life, not something to be feared.

And when I was a youngen, I didn't think about how much my life would change when I was old enough to be dragged into the darkness with my da. It wasn't the usual worries that bothered me, it was the danger that arrived with coming of age. That's what Da called it at the time. I knew I would need to step up and take over.

There was no doubt in my mind I had a duty to the club. But I convinced myself it would be when I turned eighteen, and not before that.

My da was a leader.

He had men who followed him into the flames, and they all came out on the other side. Walking around like they owned the world, even though the country was burning around them. Unscathed by what life threw at them, ignorant to the people who needed their help. The problem was, they became overconfident.

When you don't know loss, pain, or heartache, you think you are invincible.

They did.

My da convinced his men they would live forever. But that didn't happen, and he left me and Ma on our own. The memory of the war he started is still fresh in my mind. Only two years have passed since he died, and I notice how Ma still seems as if she's walkin' around in a trance.

I lift my stare to her, hoping she'll look at me, but she doesn't. As I sip my coffee, I wonder when she'll stop missin' him, if ever. She may be gettin' older, but she's still the strong woman I've always known her to be. It's Sunday; she's dressed in her favourite outfit as she gets ready to go to church. I may not be joinin' her, but she'll pray for me. It's what she tells me every week.

"I'll pray for you," her words come as she grabs her purse and glances my way. She still loves me, has hope for me, even though I may not believe in what she does. I don't go to church or pray. I gave up on that a long time ago. But the way my ma looks at me is nothin' short of a miracle—her expression filled with love, with affection she shouldn't feel. But she does. One thing about her is she's stubborn. Must be where I get it from.

"Aye." I chuckle. "No need. You know I'm goin' straight to hell," I tell her. It's somethin' I believe with every fibre of my being. When I was thirteen, I remember standin' and singing some feckin' hymn that meant nothin' to me. It was part of the service, but when I looked up, my gaze caught the priest's, and he smirked. It was as if he knew I was tainted, and he made the sign of the cross.

Ma used to call me her wee monster. I was a nightmare growing up, and even now, as an adult, the name stuck. Which is why it's my road name. I've come into my own, and I'm proud of it.

She tuts at me. "Ach, don't you go talkin' like that now." She leans up onto her tiptoes to press a kiss to my cheek. "He knew what was comin'," Ma says in a soft voice. "You just make sure to walk through that door safe tonight," she tells me before she steps out into the early morning sunshine. It's a beautiful day. You'd never think I'm about to step into my father's shoes. I didn't want it. I was happy being the Vice President of the club, but it's the line of succession. There's too much to do without fighting what's inevitable.

Once I'm alone in the house, I wonder if I'll ever see the disdain on Ma's face when I become President. It's not a life she wanted for me, but there is no choice. I can't walk away from a legacy. Her words ring in my ears. It's somethin' she's always said to me before walkin' out of the house.

Makin' my way to the small office I set up after Da died, I shut the door, and I settle in behind the desk. We have a meetin' later, and I have ta get my shite in order. Opening the clubs on the Main Street this weekend has been grand. But we need more income. There's only one way I can see to get that, but I'm not prepared to deal drugs. Weapons, maybe. I'm about to call my VP, Rebel, when gunshots ring through the air.

Panic twists in my gut because I realise I didn't hear the engine on Ma's car startin'. Crouching down, I creep to the office door and down the hallway before another round of gunfire hits the windows of our home. The place I grew up in. Even though I have the clubhouse and all that comes with it, farmland that spans hundreds of acres just outside Belfast, I've always stayed home. Being in the city energises me.

When I reach the living room, I pull my gun from the leather holster and get to my knees. I can't take any chances when it comes to violence, when it comes to being under attack. I'm alone here, and if someone did want to get in, I can only fight so much. Being outnumbered has never bothered me, not even now, but the thought of Ma being out there alone, it's got me pushing to my feet. I lean against the wall beside our front door and breathe in deeply.

Listening for any more noise outside, I close my eyes and focus. I wait a couple of minutes before I pull open the front door, hiding behind the wooden surface, and show my gun first. Silence greets me when I do, which means they're gone, or they're waitin' on me to walk out.

But when no shots come, I step out into the line of fire with my heart beating a rhythm against my chest. My ribs ache from the thrum, and as I make my way onto the small porch where Ma and Da used to sit every evening, I take in the destruction in front of me.

In death there is silence.

It's only when I reach the wee garden, do I see it. Blood. I've never seen so much mayhem in one small area before. Droppin' my gun, I race out into the street, forgetting there are men out here who want me dead. I find my mother's car still in the same place she parked it yesterday, with holes all through the doors, the one side completely fuckin' obliterated.

It's not that which has me fallin' to my knees, though, it's the ol' lady in the driver's seat. She's not breathing. The window has shattered, glass everywhere, and her mouth hangs open while her eyes are wide with shock as she stares out into the abyss.

Pain shatters me. The twisting in my gut only tightens when I reach for her neck and place two fingers against it. The wrinkled flesh against my fingertips doesn't do anything because there's no heartbeat. Her breath doesn't come. There isn't a final gasp or a last word.

"Ma," I call to her, but it's in vain because I know she won't answer. She'll never answer me again. There'll never be another prayer sent to heaven for me. Not that I believe in it, but she offered a comfort when she said it. All her life she prayed for me. She wanted what was best for me. The woman stood by me when she learned I would become President of the Royal Bastards. She didn't tell me to leave. Ma loved me unconditionally, as I did her.

Love comes with a price.

I pull open the door, and my mother's body slumps toward me. Catching her, I blink away the tears that threaten. They burn, and I want nothing more than to give my life for hers. The bastards were after me. Whoever they were, they wanted me dead, but instead, they stole the last good thing in my life.

The image of her blurs, and my vision is stolen when I drop my head against hers and shut my eyes. And I do the one thing I haven't done in years–I pray. Never once did I think I'd be on my knees, calling out to a God who long ago had forsaken me, beggin' for him to bring my mother to life. She always wanted me to join her in prayer. And it's in her death I finally do.

I don't know how long I'm on my knees, but when I feel a hand on my shoulder, I glance up, the sun momentarily blinding me. He steps into the light, and I see Rebel staring down at me. The look on his face tells me everything I need to know.

Today I become the President.

And today, I make a vow of revenge.

CHAPTER ONE

Monster

Present Day

Our warehouse is abandoned. Outside Belfast, it sits in an area where most sane folk don't venture. They know it's owned by the Royal Bastards MC, and they know to respect our privacy. The peelers don't bother comin' out here either, because they know they'll get paid generously to turn a blind eye. We don't give them a reason to pin anythin' on us while we help them clean up the city. It's the only reason they allow us to do as we please.

Flickin' the blade open, I smile when the man before me cowers. I've spent a long time watchin' these bastards. I want to find the man who killed my ma, and I know I'm getting closer. Today is the first time in years I feel I'm right on the edge, and I'm about to uncover the truth.

Since that day, holding my ma's dead body in my arms, I'd been on a mission. Nothin' coulda stopped me from this path I've chosen. I don't know if she woulda been angry with me, watchin' me torture and kill, but I need this. My blood boils every time I find out more information.

The confessions of fifty dead men still replay in my mind. It was the Irish mafia. Even though they came for me, for my family, I don't know why. Da isn't around to offer me answers, so I'm goin' ta have to find them myself.

"P-please," the bastard begs as he looks up at me with watery eyes. They shimmer in the darkness. Nighttime is when I work best. The shadows hide all sorts of acts. I've seen them all. As the President of the Royal Bastards MC, Belfast Chapter, I've taken the club my da left behind, and I ensured it didn't fall apart. The men didn't trust me at first, I was a youngen with no experience.

But now, ten years down the line, I'm the feckin' king.

"Snivelin' won't get you free from this," I tell him. "You give me answers, and I'll think about endin' you quick." I lean in and get in his face. Allowing the blade to slide against his cheek, I smile when a sliver of blood trickles from the cut. His pained hiss makes me chuckle. "That isn't the worst thing we can do to you," I continue. "Now, tell me where to find the bastard in charge."

I should be shittin' myself in fear of finding Bragan. But I ain't because the moment I do, I'm goin' ta kill him. My focus has been to avenge Ma's death. I left fear back on the street the day she died. Nothing prepared me for seeing her shot like that. And I've seen some bad shite in my life.

"I-I-I don't know," the bastard spits out, blood dripping from his mouth as he looks up at me. I can tell we've gotten all we can out of him, which only means one thing. No witnesses, nobody to run back to their leader to tell on me.

I don't think twice about pressing the blade against his neck. The blood that slowly seeps from the wound drenches my fingers. It turns the metal red. Death comes to us all—there is no escaping it. And when you least expect it, you'll end up six feet under.

"Any last words?" I can't stop the smile from appearing on my face. I no longer feel anything. I'm numb to emotion, to guilt or pain, or even fear. I allowed heartbreak to hold me hostage for so long, but as the years went by, I shoved all those human feelings into a box and locked it up tight. I'm no longer a man. I've become a monster.

"P-please, Cathal," he begs, using my given name. It's the one my mother gifted me when I was born. Taken from the Celtic elements that bring together a meaning of battle and rule. I was brought into this world with violence in my veins. It ran through my blood, and it has become synonymous with how I run the club.

"Tie his hands down," I order Rebel who smirks when he steps forward. My VP has an addiction to torture. I've watched him smile as he's sliced a man's mouth from ear to ear. There are things going on inside his head that worry me.

Once the bastard's wrists are bound to the arms of the chair, I place my little device firmly over his hand.

"I-I-I can't tell you anything," he informs me, but I know it's a lie. He can give me all the answers I need, but he won't because he knows he's goin' ta die. So, whether he confesses now, or not, he'll end up the same way.

The blade hangs waiting to be dropped. It looks like a mini version of a guillotine. But this one doesn't decapitate; it chops off fingers one by one.

"Now," I start. "Where's Bragan?" My focus is on his watery gaze. The man is crying, he's nearing his limit, and when he reaches it, I'll push way past it if he doesn't give me what I want. The only men I respect, I will die for, are my brothers. Anyone else means nothing to me. I've lived my life like that, with loyalty running through my veins. I won't change. Nobody else will ever change me.

"I-I don't know," he sputters, and I tug on the string, which lets the guillotine drop, and his index finger falls to the ground in a wet splat—the concrete stained in red. "Fuck!"

"Like I said before, I'm not goin' ta feck around," I tell him. "Where is Bragan?"

He looks up at me, the plea in his expression evident. The bastard wants me to release him. He wants to ask me for mercy, but he knows that's not possible. I don't show anyone mercy, not when it comes to the fucker who killed Ma.

I've spent my life searching, and I won't stop. All

the soldiers who work for the mob will pay with their lives. It doesn't matter if they give me the information or not. There's no such thing as leniency when it comes to criminals.

I want to laugh. Some would call the Royal Bastards criminals. But we don't go after innocent people. Those we do torture, those we do kill, they deserve it. As much as I hated Da for pushing me into this life, I vowed I wouldn't turn out like he did. And I wouldn't be six feet under before my fiftieth birthday. As I child, I looked at him and fear gripped me. I was scared I would become exactly like him.

I didn't.

I'm better.

That's what I tell myself. My father enjoyed putting the fear of God in people. He told me once I'd die if I didn't force respect, but it's not something you can force. It's earned. And I vowed to live by my own rules. I may not have a whole lot of morals when it comes to violence, but I do have my limits. I have my conscience, which ensures I don't live with guilt.

"Address," I say as I tug on the wire, which drops the blade once more, and his middle finger plops onto the concrete. A wet spatter of crimson. Blood no longer scares me. Having it on my hands, being drenched in it, I bask in the evidence of what I've done. "If you don't give it to me, I'll gladly cut you to pieces, and then, while you're still alive and breathing, I'll take acid to yer flesh," I tell him without a hint of humour. What I enjoy is making bad men pay. I may not be a feckin' angel, but by God, I'm a man with integrity.

"M-M-M-McCarthy S-S-Street," he chokes out, pain creasing his features. "The house is big enough you wouldn't miss it." His words are more confident now. He looks up at me as if I'm a saviour. I'm not. I'm the fuckin' reaper. "Please, Cathal," Moore begs. He's worked for Bragan for a number of years. One of our informants brought his name to us. He was easy enough to find. Perhaps he was confident his connection to the Irish mob would keep him safe. It won't.

I pull on all the remaining strings, and the rest of his fingers fall free from his hand. The blood-curdling scream echoes in the empty warehouse as I step back and survey my work. He's lost all his fingers on his left hand. His right hand is broken.

He looks over at me, and I note that the pain is takin' it's toll on him. But I can't allow him to live. It's not part of the plan. None of Bragan's men will live. The whole feckin' mob will go down, and it'll be by my hand.

"When you get to hell," I tell him then, "make sure you keep space for Bragan, because he'll be joinin' you soon."

I pull out my Glock and aim it at his head. The shock that's painted on his face tells me he wasn't expectin' me to kill him. But he can't live. I pull the trigger to put the bastard out of his misery.

The sound of the gunshot echoes through the air. Lowering the weapon, I turn to find Sully enter. He's been the Cleaner for a few years, and he's good at what he does. I wouldn't want anyone else doin' this for me. He drops his cigarette on the ground, before glancin' around. It's a mess.

"Monster," he says with a smile as he grabs the gloves from his rucksack. Ready to work, he has a bag of tricks which will cleanse this place of the violence.

"Clean this mess up," I tell him as he dons his gloves. The thick black plastic will ensure he doesn't get his hands dirty. The man is a feckin' professional when it comes to messes.

I step out of the warehouse into the weak autumn sunshine. It's only goin' ta get colder from here on out. Rebel saunters up to me. My VP has been with me for as long as I can remember. We grew up as youngens in the streets of Belfast. When bombs were easily bought and sold, where violence was as normal as the feckin' sun rising. Most didn't witness what we did. They went about their daily lives, but we knew what it was like to have death on our doorstep.

"The fecker give the address up?" he asks me when he stops in front of me. He offers me a smoke, which I accept with a nod.

"Aye." I pull in a lungful of air once I've lit the cigarette, and I blow out a cloud before saying, "I think we're goin' ta need to pay Bragan a visit today."

"I've asked Racer to get on the weapons run," he tells me.

The club runs some guns for the Italian mafia in London. They contacted us a couple of years ago to help keep tabs on shipments that come into Ireland. I wouldn't want to start shite with an outfit like theirs, so I agreed. The money is good, and we need the income.

"I think we need to tell them to slow down the stock comin' in," I tell Rebel. "That's two feckin' shipments in a month. If we've got eyes on us from the Irish mob, I don't want them to see connections with the Italians."

"Bragan will be dead soon."

"Aye, but he's still got men in Dublin, and Belfast. We may not have all their names yet, but those feckers will be watching. I can't guarantee we'll be safe." The one thing I always make sure of is that my men aren't in harm's way, at least for the most part. Our lives are a constant stream of danger, but if we can stop it, then we do.

"Understood," Rebel says. He kills his smoke and looks up at me. "It's coming on to the anniversary."

I didn't want to think about it today. My focus was on finding the man who has been the bane of my existence for most of my adult life. The one who took my family from me.

"Which is why I need to find the fecker," I tell my VP.

He knows that the anniversary of my mother's death is tough for me. It's coming up next week, and I have to go through the feckin' heartache again. If I can tell her I've avenged her death, it would be a weight off my shoulders. I don't want her lookin' down on me, watchin' me kill when it's not for the benefit of innocents. She needs to know her son was brought up right, that I remember the values she taught me.

Even though I chose my da's way of life, it's Ma who made me the man I am today.

"We will," Rebel assures me.

Now that we have an address, it's goin' ta make life a lot easier. I know the house Moore was talkin' about. It's one I've looked at so many times before, unknowingly. An estate that was housing a killer. Most of the mob homes have deeds with names that don't belong to the members. It's their way of keeping the bastards safe. I've hated the mob for as long as I can remember. I've heard the stories about them, how they'll hurt innocent women and children. The wee ones payin' for the sins of their fathers without knowing what's happenin'.

"We need to get to that house," I tell Rebel.

Confusion is clear on his face as he looks at me before Rebel warns, "We need a plan before we go in guns blazin'."

"If we waste time, he'll have the opportunity to get away."

"I'm not saying we shouldn't go there today, but we need backup. Let's at least get the rest of the brothers. They can bring the van," he says then, and I realise he's right. I can't afford to fuck this up. We should make sure when we walk into that house, we're the ones with the advantage. Bragan isn't goin' ta be sitting there alone. He's goin' ta have men surrounding him. He'll ensure his security has been amped up.

I look at Rebel. "Fine. Make the call."

The man is right. I shouldn't run into this without a clear plan. But it's been years, and I'm ready to finally put an end to this need for revenge. I've always wanted to see the man who killed my mother. I want to look him in the eye and make sure he never hurts anyone else again. And now he's within reaching distance, I'm even more anxious.

When I'm on edge, I usually have to take a step back and think things through. But when you're traumatised, sometimes the only thing you can do is run headfirst into a situation. That's what my father used to do, and I swore I wouldn't put my men through the same thing.

When I was younger, I thought Da was the hero. He always made himself out to be. But I slowly realised as I got older, that's not the way to do things.

"Let's get back to the clubhouse. We'll have a meeting this afternoon and get the plan set out." I relay the order to the brothers before hopping on my bike and revving the engine. It's time to go home, get the plan ironed out, and then we'll attack.

CHAPTER TWO

Miren

Graduating with a bachelor's degree from university has been my sole focus since I decided what I wanted to do with my life. It took years to choose a subject I was happy with. I'm not yet qualified, I still have a few years to go before I can see patients, but once I get a doctorate, I'll be able to do something meaningful with my life.

I know my mother would have most certainly pushed me in another direction, but when I told her my desire was to help people, she appeased me by agreeing to let me study psychology. I didn't follow in her footsteps of the corporate world as such. To this day, I'm not entirely sure what my mother does, but I do know she owns businesses across the globe. We've travelled far and wide, but I would like to find an internship while I complete my studies.

London is filled with tourists today as I make my way through the throng. Covent Garden is packed, and I'm ready to get home and hide in my bedroom until Christmas arrives. But, August is my favourite time of the year as the leaves turn yellow and orange and the city becomes an autumn wonderland. As I grab a takeaway coffee, I offer smiles to those I pass. I do prefer my quiet time, but there are moments of magic when it comes to the season change in the big city.

Tonight, we'll have dinner with some of my mother's colleagues. I've always been proud of her. As a female in a male-dominated world, she's made a name for herself. She's respected by her peers. Banking, finance, and transport, she's held her own amongst the sharks, and now that she's talking about possibly retiring early, I wonder what that means for me. Granted, I'm ready to leave home now. At twenty-two, I want to get my own place. I've just been rather lazy at searching for something I like.

As I make my way toward the tube station, a cold shiver trickles down my spine, but when I glance over my shoulder, trying to find the haunting eyes I'm pretty sure are watching me, I'm dizzied by the amount of people.

I should really tell Mum I've had this strange feeling I have of being watched, but I don't want to bother her. She'll only worry, and when she does find out, I'll probably have bodyguards following me around. My mother has always said her work can be dangerous. That people may seek revenge on her business decisions. It doesn't truly make sense to me, but I've obeyed her directions and rules all my life.

I don't go out alone at night. I'm careful about what I share online. And when I do head to a party or dinner, I'm always with friends. Mum usually gets a private car to pick me up and take me home. But tonight, I wanted to be *normal* and jump on the tube. It's busy enough that I don't particularly feel afraid.

By the time I'm on the train, I'm surrounded by people, and the shadow that's been following me seems to have disappeared. Perhaps it's my imagination. I shouldn't let things get to me, but learning about the human mind and how it works, I *see* more than other people do. I tend to read others, mostly because I'm intrigued to know what makes them tick. I love to assess and delve deep into their minds to find out what scares them, what worries them, and most times, it's something new.

I've always enjoyed people watching. That's how I would spend my time in parks, coffee shops, even at school. I would try to garner what I could about someone just by taking in their responses to situations. That's what brought me to where I am today.

When my station stop appears, I step off and follow the crowd as we make our way to the exit. It's not far to walk from here, and I turn left the moment I get onto the pavement. The house is only a few streets away, but still, the nervous feeling that's been haunting me attacks once more, and I stop in the middle of the crowd.

As people pass me by, they don't take note of me. Nobody notices anyone in London. The city is busy; there isn't really time to stop and think. No moment where you even look at a stranger. When I no longer feel eyes on me, I turn and head down towards Chelsea, where our semi-detached townhouse is situated. Once inside, I breathe deeply. My pulse riots against my chest, and I know I should tell my mother about what happened.

It's become the norm for me to feel as if someone is watching me. And if I don't tell her, and something happens, she'll feel guilty. I can't have that happen. Setting my purse down on the table at the entrance, I decide to go to the kitchen first. It's empty, but I grab a water and choose to wait till dinner before I talk to her. She's probably in her office, and I don't like disturbing her when she's working.

I'm about to take the stairs to the first floor when I hear my mother's voice shout at someone. I've heard her angry before, but this is different. Ignoring my escape up to my room, I head toward her office instead. If she's in trouble, I should try to help.

The door is slightly ajar, and I reach for the handle, but I'm stopped in my tracks when I hear her voice again. "She's not coming to live with you." Her tone is no nonsense, and I've heard it before. Whenever I wanted to do something she didn't agree with, I'd be told directly I would be locked in my room or grounded if I disobeyed.

The silence tells me she's on a call. I wait to listen, leaning against the doorframe. My mother has many business partners, and for a moment, I'm certain she's talking about them.

But then she says, "I took her when she was a child

because I didn't need her in harm's way. You know if I'd left her with you, she wouldn't have made it past her thirteenth birthday." My chest tightens, and my heart thuds wildly against my ribs. It must be my father she's talking to.

The thing is, I haven't seen him before. I don't even know his name. When I asked my mother, time and again, she always told me was in the army. The story was that he got deployed, and never returned home. I believed her, but from what I can tell right now, she is talking to him.

"Listen to me," she says, but then doesn't continue, and I wonder if the man on the other end of the line interrupted her. If he did, he must have said something bad, because seconds later, a vase smashes to the floor, causing me to jump. I can imagine which one it is. When I was little, I always thought it was magical. A large, crystal monstrosity that shimmered as if there was glitter in it.

"You can try," Mum says. "But it's not going to work. You know why? Because she's my fucking daughter. I worked hard to put her through school, to make sure she's not a part of this organisation. She's free from the confines her grandfather set out, and I'm not about to let her walk right back into it."

For a long while it's quiet, and I close my eyes as I breathe softly. I don't want her to hear me. I can't let her know I've overheard the conversation. With delicate steps, I move away from the door and make it to the staircase before she exits her office.

"Miren," Mum's voice calls to me. "I didn't realise you were home already."

I glance over at her and smile. "I just walked in." The lie tastes like a bitter pill on my tongue, but it's the only way I can make sure she doesn't realise I've eavesdropped. "How was your day?" I ask lightly, hoping the change of thoughts racing through my mind will calm my erratic heartbeat.

If I can get to my room, I can figure out who my mother was talking to, which I can only assume is my father, though she told me he's dead.

"It's been busy," she tells me, but she doesn't meet my eye. Something I learned whilst doing my studies was anyone who can't make eye contact is hiding something. I've learned how to read people over the past four years. Even though I still have years to go before I graduate, I know for a fact what I studied so far is true. "I have a few meetings coming up this week. I may be out of town for a while, so I'd like you to make sure you're driven everywhere. Don't go out partying, please." She looks at me with worry in her eyes. "Also, I'd like you to ask Alexia to stay. Perhaps you both can do those spa weekends you enjoy so much."

"I don't understand. I thought your meetings were over for the year. You said you had booked time off for us to head to Europe for a couple of months before coming back for our annual market adventure." It's something Mum started when I was little. We would go to every market in London in November.

"Miren," she says then, and I can tell I've annoyed her by the way her face creases. "Just do as I say." Her order is clear. There won't be any debate about this, so I nod.

"Maybe we can have supper together tonight?" I ask her in the hopes that she agrees. If she does, I can finally sit down and tell her about the person following me. I'm pretty sure after hearing her conversation, it's related to whoever was on the line.

"Yes, yes," Mum says before waving a hand in the air and making her way back to her office. Something tells me she's about to open the bottle of Dunville's whiskey that sits on her liquor cabinet. Sighing, I turn and make my way up the stairs.

In my bedroom, I settle at my desk and open my laptop. There must be a way to find out who my father is. Or even if Mum has had any relationships before I was born. Opening my browser, I wonder if I could ask one of her investigators for help but decide against it. If I do, they could easily go to her and tell her what I've done. No. I need to be careful.

In the search bar, I type in my mother's name and hit Enter. Once the results load, I scroll through the websites, but nothing jumps out at me. Everything they have on Mum is from her work life. There isn't anything personal. It's as if she doesn't exist past her finance company.

Unless she changed her name. Perhaps my mother was married, and she didn't tell me. As far as I know, she and my father weren't together. I was the result of a one-night stand, but maybe I wasn't. She could have told me one story and kept the truth to herself. Seeing today how easily she lied, I wouldn't put it past her. And that's what scares me.

If Mum is hiding something, the man following me might be looking for her. Perhaps he wanted to see where I lived in order to get to my mother. The thought of that sets me on edge. I push to my feet and go to my bedroom window. From here, I can see our small, yet quiet street and try to note if anything seems amiss.

I look left and right, taking in every car, every person

strolling by, but nobody seems out of place. But then again, if someone is stalking me, they're not going to make it obvious. They won't be visible, and that makes me even more nervous.

I should go down and talk to her. Decision made, I turn away from the window. It's not giving me any answers anyway, and I make my way down the hall. Taking the steps one at a time, I walk to my mother's office and push open the door. But I'm startled to find she's not there. I'm pretty sure I saw her coming this way earlier.

"Mum!" I call out, hoping not to startle her. But there's no response.

I go in search of her in the kitchen, living room, and then down to the basement where she keeps her wine collection, but she's not there. Her car was still parked out on the street, which is strange. If she were to go out, she would drive. My mother doesn't trust anyone to drive her anywhere. It's one of the reasons we argue about me travelling to school and back. As much as I appreciate our driver, I would love to have my own car. For some reason though, she's never liked the idea of me driving alone.

I search the whole house, even the attic, finding no sign of my mum. Panic sets in as I pull out my phone and hit dial on her number. It rings, but when she doesn't answer, the call is sent to voicemail. Her voice comes through telling me to leave my name and number after the tone. I hang up and try again as I make my way down toward the entrance hall.

But it's when I hear the ringing in her office that alarm bells blare in my ears. Something is wrong. I'm sure of it. In her private sanctuary, I search for the device and find it in a drawer of her desk. I take it out and set it on the desktop. My gaze catches onto the folder that's perfectly nestled in the compartment, and I pull it out. On the front is the word **PRIVATE** in bold, capital letters, while the rest of the cover is blank.

My fingers tremble as my legs give way, and I flop onto her leather chair. The soft cushion under me offers support, but when I open the folder and my focus lands on the photo attached to pages of documents, my heart stutters.

My mother lied to me. She's been lying to me since I was little. Emotions coil in my gut, tightly knotting in both anger and frustration, but also a hint of sadness. There, right in front of me, is a photo of my father. It's so clear that's who the man is because I look just like him.

All my life, I've wondered why my mother's bright

red curls are nothing like my wavy chocolate brown. In truth, I may have a tinge of red in my hair if I stand in the sun, but it's my pale blue-grey eyes that are nothing like her green ones. But they look exactly like the man's in the photo.

Setting it down, I focus on the information.

And that's when, for the first time in my life, I see my father's real name.

I'm about to turn the page when the hair on the back of my neck stands on end, and suddenly, there's a cloth over my mouth. I struggle with the strong hand holding it in place, but I'm no match. No matter how much I claw at the flesh, I can't fight off the attacker.

And as my lashes flutter closed, realisation dawns on me that the person who had been following me has finally caught up. That's when everything goes black.

CHAPTER THREE

Miren

When my eyes flutter open, there's a pounding in my skull. It feels as if I'd been drinking far too much alcohol and not enough water. My mind is fuzzy as I roll over and wince at the throb behind my eyes. I'm pretty sure I didn't go out partying last night. I look around at the darkened room, and reality slams right into me.

It's not my bedroom. The last thing I remember is seeing a photo of a man who I thought was my father. The memory is so clear, and his face is still ingrained in my thoughts. I never thought I would ever see him, but my mother's secrets have slowly come to light. Her lies are now revealed, and I don't know what to make of it.

Pushing to my feet, I take in my surroundings. It's not a bad bedroom. There's a lovely king-sized bed, along with heavy, suede curtains and a dresser. When I pull open the curtains, it's raining.

I'm not entirely sure where I am, but it's most certainly not London. It's still dark out, but there isn't a flickering light from my viewpoint, which means the house I'm in must be outside the city. It looks like I'm in the countryside.

I leave the curtains open as I explore the rest of the room, but there's not too much else to find. The cupboards are empty, as are the drawers in the vanity unit. The door to the actual room is locked, so no matter how much I try, I can't get out.

I shout out for help and wait, listening for any sign of life on the other side of the door, but there's nothing. No response. So, I try once more, and in the deafening silence, the only thing I can hear is my heart thudding in my ears.

I can't escape. There's no indication of who has taken me, or what they want from me. All I can be grateful for is the fact they haven't hurt me. Yet.

I'm a prisoner.

I'm even more certain now that the man responsible for this is my father. Anything else doesn't make sense. It must be who Mum was talking to when I overheard her. And the folder I found in her office was evidence enough she was never completely honest with me.

I settle back on the bed, but I'm not relaxed. Far from it. Flicking on the bedside lamp, I slip back under the covers and curl into a ball.

My mind is racing with thoughts of how I'm going to get out of here. No matter who took me, I'm not staying here. I won't agree to anything they want from me. My mother taught me to be strong, and I'm not about to let her down. She's fought for me, even though she lied. Hearing her tell the person on the other end of the phone she won't let me go to them, only strengthens my resolve.

My stomach rumbles. I'm hungry. Mum and I were meant to have dinner, but she wasn't in the office when I looked for her, and now, I'm here. In a house I've never seen before, and I don't know who took me.

Exhaustion and the headache take hold of me, and I shut my eyes in the hopes it will help ease the pain. My throat is dry. I'm thirsty, hungry, and tired. As I lie here alone, I cry. The tears slowly trickle down the side of my face onto the pillow.

And I finally allow sleep to steal me.

"Get up, *áilleacht*." A deep voice startles me awake, and I sit up before scooting back on the bed, hitting the headboard with a thud. The blankets cover me, and I tug them to my chin, wanting to hide from the man standing in the bedroom.

"Who are you?" My voice is weak, broken. My throat burns, and I can't help coughing. It feels as if there is sandpaper in my oesophagus. My chest is tight, my heartbeat thundering wildly against my ribs.

"Come, we need to go," he tells me without answering my question, but I do recognise his accent— Irish. I can't pinpoint which particular area he's from, but he's definitely not from London.

"I'm not going anywhere until you tell me who you are," I bite back, frustrated and scared.

There's no doubt about it, this man could probably kill me, but I'm not going to show my fear. He may have all the power, but I can't just ignore the fact he's a bad person. And I want answers.

"Just tell me who you are and what I'm doing here, please?" I use a softer tone, hoping this man, whoever he is, will offer some clarity.

"All those answers will be given to you downstairs," he tells me, his accent thick, and I wonder again where he's from. Or where I am.

Deciding to obey, I push off the bed and walk over to where he's standing. I'm barefoot, and I didn't see my shoes anywhere in the room. I'm resigned to the fact they've been taken, but I'm not sure why. When I reach him he grips my arm harshly and shoves me over the threshold which causes me to stumble into another waiting in the shadows.

The strange thing is, they're both in suits. Their formal attire makes me think they're bodyguards or something similar. Mum's security detail were always well dressed. Their suits tailored to fit them perfectly.

I've grown up in a world of luxury. I'm used to people perfectly poised, immaculately dressed, and what most would consider *posh*. So I wonder if my father, if it is him who's taken me, comes from wealth as well.

We make our way down a long, dimly lit hallway. The bulbs that illuminate the way offer a soft yellow glow. The walls are painted light grey, while the carpet underfoot is black. The monochrome decor is broken by the bright and colourful artwork on the walls. From what I can tell, they're all modernist paintings. When we reach the entrance hall, I recognise a few of Andy Warhol's artwork.

Downstairs is just as stark, with white walls and black tiles. No other colour, bar from the art. The one man grips my arm once more, causing me to wince, and he drags me to the right of the door. My freedom may sit just outside, but I'm not able to get to it as I'm led deeper into the house.

We get to a room that's furnished in a modern lounge suite, two large sofas of black suede, and two armchairs. They face a long, glass coffee table.

The room itself is lit in a warm glow of off-white, while the floor-to-ceiling patio doors show off the darkness beyond. A door on the opposite end of the room opens, and a man saunters in. And it's like the air is sucked out the moment he walks through. I recognise him. The man from the photo in my mother's office.

He's dressed smartly, with a dark suit clearly tailored for him. The crisp white shirt underneath is bright, a stark contrast to his jacket. And the deep green tie pops against the cotton. He looks at me with a smile curling his lips, and I'm startled at the blue-grey of his eyes. My eyes.

"Miren." He says my name as if he knows me. It's like he's uttered my name his whole life. He stops a few feet from me, and now I'm so close to the man I believe is my father, my stomach twists. I'm nervous and scared, but I'm also intrigued.

"You kidnapped me," I say out loud, and the two men behind me chuckle. I want nothing more than to turn to them and hurt them both. My arm is still smarting from where the one gripped me, and I'm certain it will leave a bruise.

"I had you brought home," the man with the familiar colour eyes says. His accent thick with an Irish brogue. I think back to my mum's stories of her childhood, and I know she was born in Northern Ireland. But because we never visited there, I hadn't really come across people with the similar accent to the man before me.

"I was home," I tell him. "But I was stolen from my home and brought," I mutter, looking around, "to your house. A place I don't know and would never consider home."

There's a glint in his eye, a smirk on his lips, and he tips his head to the side as he regards me. I can tell this man isn't perturbed by my insolence. He looks amused rather than angry. His shoulders lift in a shrug when he turns and seats himself in one of the armchairs. His left leg crossing over his right as he leans back and settles his hands on the arms of the chair.

Crossing my arms over my chest, I ask, "What am I doing here?"

"I told you," he says. "You're home now." He watches me for a long moment, and I'm more angry than fearful now. "I suggest you sit." He tips his head towards the sofa, and for a moment, I want to disobey and ignore his gesture, but one of the men behind me grips my arm and tugs me toward it.

Soon enough, I'm sitting, facing my captor.

"Who are you?"

I don't flinch. I don't cower. My shoulders are squared in a fake show of confidence. I'm far from it. My stomach is in knots at the moment, and I'm worried I may be sick if he tries to touch me. But my bravado pays off when he smiles again.

"My name is Patrick," he tells me. "I've known yer mother for most of her life." My heart catapults at his confession. "And as much as I do think she's a rather lovely woman, she's disobeyed me far too much. I'm not a man who submits."

"I don't know what you mean." This time, I'm confused. Why would he submit to my mother? And then her conversation on the phone rings in my ears. She told him he cannot have me, that I'm not able to visit him. So instead of trying to coax her to allow it, he's stolen me.

"You'll learn soon enough, sweetheart," he tells me as he reaches into his jacket pocket and pulls out a phone. He taps the screen a few times before looking back at me. "So, tell me all about you."

Instead of giving him what he wants, I question instead, "Where is my mother?"

"Let me make something clear, sweetheart," he says before leaning forward. His elbows resting on his knees. "I don't take kindly to rudeness. And I am far from a patient man. If I want something, I take it."

"You steal it," I bite back. Seconds later, he's in my face, and my cheek is stinging with the harsh swat he lands on me.

"Don't you dare disrespect me," he grumbles deeply, his voice vibrating through his chest. His hands fist at his sides, and I shut my eyes as I await another attack, but it doesn't come. I open my eyes and watch as he rises to full height.

"Why am I here?" I ask, noticing how he fists his hands, but he doesn't strike me again. I am pretty sure he's ready to hit me, to hurt me, but I am his daughter. I have no doubt about it. The resemblance is far too close.

"Your mother kept you hidden from me," he tells

me as he turns and makes his way to the cabinet sitting across the room. It's filled with shimmering bottles of alcohol. "She's ensured I didn't get to see my little girl grow up. And I'm done obeying her rules."

"If you knew I was alive, that I was born, you could have searched for me," I tell him with frustration in my tone. "I asked her about you, and she told me you were dead." As angry as I am at being kidnapped, when he turns around, I can read the anguish in his face. The man has done something bad, something wrong, but I have a feeling he's only a father wanting to meet his daughter.

"There were many times over the years I wanted to come for ye," he tells me before he lifts his tumbler and takes a sip of the ochre liquid. "But I wanted ye to have a grand life, and she promised me ye would. There are so many things at play here, Miren."

"I don't understand."

"Would ye like a drink? My girl is old enough now to enjoy a drink with her old man," he tells me. Those eyes that match mine hold hope. It's strange to see a man like him so pained. I have no doubt in my mind he's strong, dangerous, and the boss of the men he rules over. I'm pretty sure my father is a mobster from the way he seems to command attention, and from what I read in the file before I was taken, Mum hinted at his criminal activities.

"No, thank you," I tell him with a shake of my head. "I just need to know if my mum is okay."

"Aye," he says with a smile. "Ye mam is a strong woman. She's not goin' ta let herself get killed, I can assure you of that, Miren." He moves through the room slowly before sitting on the armchair once more. "And I could never hurt her."

"But you could have me kidnapped?"

"Is it kidnapping when it's yer own kin?" he challenges me with a smirk as he rests his right ankle on his left knee. "I think you're looking at this the wrong way, sweetheart," he says. "I'm here to care for you. To show you I'm not an absentee father. I may not have been there throughout yer younger years, but I want to be here now."

"What makes you think I need you now?"

"Nothing." He shrugs as if it's the last thing he would consider. He smiles and a glint in his eye sparkles. I wonder briefly if my mother ever loved him. To walk away from a man whose child you're carrying can't be easy. And yet, my mum did it. It doesn't make sense to me.

"I just want to go home. That's all."

He chuckles. "I wish ye could, sweetheart," he says. "But you're here to tell me everything about ye ma's work. Living with her, I'm sure there have been times you've come across colleagues of hers."

Confusion now furrows my brows. My mother's work has never been topic of conversation between me and her. She kept her work private. If he thinks I can offer insight, then he's sorely mistaken. "I know nothing about what she does. I've spent my life being kept in the dark about her business. Mum has meetings away from the house, and if she does bring any of her partners home for dinner, or a party, they don't talk about work."

Patrick tips his head to the side as he regards me. "Now, I just don't believe that. Because surely she would've said something to ye."

"I can promise you, she's never said a word."

Frustration creases his expression, and his jaw ticks as he glares at me. Then he glances at the two men who are standing idly by and waiting instruction. "Take her to the basement."

"What? No!"

I'm gripped harshly by one of the guards, and even though I try to fight, it's no use. I'm dragged from the room, my eyes on my father as he watches. The room

I'm dumped in this time isn't as pretty as the last. It's nowhere near a room—it's a cell. And once the heavy metal door clicks, I'm left in the dark.

I don't know how much time passes until the door opens and I'm dragged out of the cell. The man holding me can lift me without breaking a sweat. He takes me down a dark hallway, and we enter another dimly lit room, which I notice has chains on the walls and a metal chair right in the middle.

He plops me down and begins binding my ankles to the chair legs, while my arms are forced behind me and tied with cuffs.

Patrick saunters in and smiles at me. I want to claw his eyes out. Anger and hatred burn their way through me. "I want you to answer some very important questions, Miren." His voice echoes in the room. The man who brought me here stands to the side, ready for an order from his boss.

"I told you, I don't know anything," I tell him, and a hand slams against the side of my face.

"I want names, all the names of the colleagues yer mam brought into that house," Patrick says, his tone so light and carefree it's as if he's talking about the weather.

"I told you I don't know," I scream, but it's no use.

Each time I respond honestly, the man hits me. His hand stings against my cheek which causes me to wince in pain. The blood trickling into my mouth from my split lip coats my tongue. And I'm convinced I'll most probably die here.

The guard pulls a knife out of a shoulder holster and brings it to my neck. The sleek blade bites into my skin as I look up at Patrick. A devil with a sinister smile.

"I'll get the truth out of you," he tells me, "one way or another."

He turns and walks away, and the warm liquid dribbling down my neck into my cleavage is evidence the bastard has cut me. I don't know what else to do but cry as I'm taken back to my cell. I have a feeling this isn't over, not by a long shot.

CHAPTER FOUR

Monster

Each day that passes makes me anxious. We're so close, yet still so far. As much as I want to avenge my mother's killer, I know I must do it with a level head. I've never been known to have patience, but for her, I'll do this the right way.

When Tye, our tech expert, looked into Bragan, there were things that didn't make sense. His private plane was out of the country, so instead of making our way to the address Moore gave us, we waited. The plan is to go straight to the house the moment I know he's there. The man has to be within my reach when I attack, because if he isn't, the whole raid will be fruitless.

Since I have Tye tracking his whereabouts, I can focus on the shipment of weapons coming in from Europe. The Italians have been working with us for years, and I have to make sure they're happy. The more they send our way, the more income we have. And that ensures my brothers have the money to enjoy their lives. We all have different pasts. None of them are from wealth, though. What we have we've worked for. And I believe it's what brings us together. We're a family, not by blood, but by loyalty.

I make my way through the clubhouse, where some of the brothers are milling around, waiting for their old ladies. I find Tye, along with Rebel and Racer, sitting in the lounge on the sofa with a few of the club whores who hang around just to get attention. I can't help but shake my head. Tye and Racer are single, but Rebel has his eyes on one of our girls. He hasn't yet made a move, and I wonder if he'll ever tell her he's in love with her. He may deny it, but it's clear as day whenever she's close. His gaze follows her around like a magnet.

"I'm headin' out to the harbour," I tell them. "Need to meet with Venier. Once I have the shipment times, we'll make our plans for the weekend. I reckon we'll keep a few men here to make sure the women are safe."

"Need me to come along?" Rebel asks. As my VP, I would usually have him riding with me, but for now, I need some time to think. Even though I have managed to run the club all these years without losing my mind, it feels as if now that Bragan is so close, I'm more anxious than usual. And a long ride out to the docks will sort my thoughts out.

Shaking my head, I tell him, "Nah, I'll be all right." I turn and make my way out of the house. It's the only place I can let down my guard, and even then, it's still a concern to let anyone too close. My brothers know me, but I still keep things to myself. Ma taught me when I was younger to never let anyone see yer cards while you're playing. If they do, they'll be able to knock you down. They'll win, and you'll end up the loser. And I refuse to lose this time. I can't. Not for me, my brothers, nor for Ma who I know is watchin' down on me.

Da did that. He was too much of a prideful bastard, and it ended up with him being killed. He didn't think about the future, about his family. But then again, he didn't see us as a family. He was far too focused on the club. Our home wasn't a place he spent his nights in. There's no doubt he was fuckin' every club whore he could get his hands on. And when I realised my father wasn't a hero, but a savage, I lost respect for him. Which is why I never want to end up like that. End up in the grave.

With the rumble of my bike filling my ears, I allow myself to think back to the day we got the news. When my father was murdered in cold blood.

The knock on the door has Ma panicking. She's always told me if it's early morning or late night, it can never be good news. Same with the telephone ringing. She insists on keeping the landline. I don't know why. I've tried showing her how to use a mobile phone, but she's refused. Technology is the devil. At times, I think she's right. But at twenty-five, I'm more connected to it than I thought I would be.

I'm shrugging on my jacket when I hear Ma wail. The agony in the sound twists at my chest like a knife slicing through me. Racing from my room, I rush into the lounge where the front door stands open, and on the threshold are two of my father's men.

"What's happenin'?" I ask, looking from Ma to them. The expression on their faces tells me what's going on before I have a chance to speak. I go to my mother and hold her. The sobs that tumble from her are heart-wrenching. "What's gone on?"

"Yer da wanted to ride out and talk to those feckers down south," Hag tells me. The man looks like he's had a tough life. One day, Da called him haggard, and the shortened version of his name stuck. He wears his patch proudly, but I wonder if he ever hated my father for the moniker.

"Where is he?"

"We tried to stop him, but he and a few of the new patch-ins went anyway." This comes from Jonesy. The man is always high or drunk. I'm not even sure how the feck he gets on a bike, but for the first time in years, he seems to be sober. He looks at me with guilt written all over his face, and I know what's happened. Da has got it in his head that he's invincible. I have a feeling that's just been proven wrong.

"Go," I tell them before leading my ma to the sofa. I sit her down and crouch so we're eye level. Seeing the heartbreak in her eyes is enough to force my decision to never fall in love. It brings about pain, nothing more than that. I've watched for years how my mother loved Da. But all he did was take advantage. He didn't truly love her. His club came before she did, before I did.

"He's..." Her voice is a whimper, which crushes my heart. I've never considered myself a ma's boy, but she's everything to me. *"He's gone."* The two words that once again shatter Ma more than I've ever seen. All my life she's never allowed her emotions to show. The only time Ma has shed tears was

when she heard news about children being slain in bombings. But now, she's slowly breaking before me. I've never seen her truly sob like this. I didn't think she would break, but when she looks up at me, I see the resolve slowly clearing her tears. "I don't want you to be like him," she tells me. "Promise me, one day when you're running that damn club he loved so much, you'll also love yer family."

I offer her a sad smile. "Ma, I doubt I'll be gettin' a family."

"Ach." She swats at me. "Don't you be talking like that now. You're a good lad, and I know you'll find a colleen who'll make you see love is worth it." Using the slang term for girl, which is colleen, Ma grins when I smile.

"Is it?" I ask honestly.

All I've seen of love is the pain and frustration Ma has been through. Aye, there were times she smiled, but they were few and far between all the anguish.

"Cathal O'Connor, don't you talk like that," she tells me, and slowly, tears still trickle from her eyes.

This is goin' ta be a long road. She's not goin' ta heal overnight. And that makes me angry. He did this. Anger surges through me like an electric current racing through my veins. He's hurt Ma. I don't care about myself. I can survive the loss of a parent who was never there, but she's loved him for most of her life. Married at seventeen, he's been the only constant in her life. I may have come along after, but the love you hold for yer soul mate is different. It's life changing.

"You understand that I don't want this heartbreak for you. Seein' you like this, it hurts me more than you can imagine. He did this. He chose a life where he was in danger all the time."

"Aye," she says with a nod. "But when you love someone dearly, there's no changing how you feel, darlin'. He may not have been perfect, but love doesn't ask for perfection."

Ma has always given me advice. Sometimes it wasn't wanted, but I always took onboard what she told me. The woman is a saint, and for her to put up with both Da and me, she's certainly had her hands full. I'm nowhere near as bad as some of my mates, but I can be difficult. I've put my hand up numerous times to admit it.

"I love you, Cathal," she tells me then. "Don't ever forget, no matter what you do, to make sure you're proud of the act, proud of the outcome."

"As long as you're proud of me, Ma. That's all that matters," I say instead, ignoring the fact there are things I've done over the past few years I'm not exactly happy with. I've made stupid choices, and I know I should pray for my sins. But the church has never been a friend. And as I sit with my mother, allowing her to cry into my chest, I know this moment is the only one that matters. I'm able to offer her some small amount of comfort.

When I pull into a parking space at the pier, I kill the engine and swing my leg over the bike and straighten up. The memory of losin' my pa is still fresh in my mind when I make my way to the sleek, black cars parked close to the offices.

I find a couple of the guards standing at the door. They offer a nod of greeting before one of them opens the office and I step inside. I've known these men for years. As much as I trust them, I'm also wary.

When I find Judah Venier inside, I'm not surprised. He's slowly been taking over the organisation from his pa. The man is a ruthless, calculated businessman, a Boss, while Judah as his Underboss is learning from the best.

"Venier," I greet him as he offers me his hand. We shake in greeting before I say, "I need to know the new times and dates for all shipments. It seems we have someone trying to undercut us."

"My father explained the issues you've been having," he tells me. "I'll ensure that nobody intercepts any communication between us. I think it's best we meet face-to-face until the problem has been dealt with."

"Aye, are you sendin' men here?"

He nods. "I'll be overseeing most of the future

shipments. My father has given me the go ahead to take over once he steps down. It means I'm going to have to get my hands dirty."

"That's not like any of the other bosses I've ever met," I respond with a chuckle. "Most of them would rather their soldiers or Capos deal with shit like this."

"True. But I don't want to be like them. Have you ever thought about taking over and wanting to be completely different to those who've come before?" He's deadly serious. I can't help but respect him and his choice.

I tip my head. "Aye, I have, and since I stepped up to take over RBMC, I've done it the way I wanted, not how everyone thought I should."

Judah may be ten years younger than me, but he has a competent head on his shoulders. At twenty-five, I recall not being as responsible as the lad in front of me. Far from it to be fair. I enjoyed the danger that came with being part of the club. Even though it led me into some dark and precarious situations. But then I realised the more I put myself in danger, there wouldn't be a club to come home to.

Judah looks at me with a smile. "Then you'll understand why I need to do this."

"Aye, no bother. I'll support yer choices, as long as

cash flow doesn't stop, and work doesn't dry up."

He smiles. "I can promise you one thing, Cathal, it's not something I would do to a trusted confidante of my father. He's taken years to build the respect from every person he's worked with, and I won't step in and butcher that."

"Then we won't have any bother," I tell him. If we're getting our shipments, and our payments are coming in, I don't give a feck about who I work with. Granted, I won't lower my morals for anyone, but I know the Veniers, and they may be mafia, but they have a code that I believe in myself. It's the only reason I agreed to the partnership. They may deal in weapons, but they never venture into the sordid side of it. No women, no children. And that's something I can stand behind.

Judah turns to the briefcase sitting on the table and flicks it open. Inside is a shiny laptop that he boots up. Soon enough, we're going through the information for each shipment. The next one is expected in a few days, which we'll be ready for.

I scan the dates and times. We'll be getting shipments every two weeks. Which means we can stock up the warehouse and get the guns delivered south. We have buyers from all over the country, including Dublin. Once they're paid up, we ride to the border and meet them for the handover. It's the only thing about my father's business I kept going.

I glance at Judah. "They all come in at midnight?"

Judah nods. "Yeah, I wanted to make sure we wouldn't be disturbed in the process of unloading the goods. And most of the men prefer working at night."

"That's no bother for us. We'll be here. I'll make sure the whole crew is with us. If we need the backup, I'd rather have them on standby than waitin' for them." I watch as he hits send on the email that will go through to mine and Tye's inboxes. Once we sit down tonight at church, I'll get all the men up to speed.

"Well, I suppose it's all settled. First ship arrives this coming weekend."

I nod. "Aye, we'll be here."

We say our goodbyes, and I know that no matter what happens, I'll be able to provide for the brothers. We have the club, which brings in a decent income, and soon enough, we plan to open another.

I'm about to start the bike when my phone buzzes.

When I pull it from my pocket, I find Father Donahue's name flashing on the screen. I haven't spoken to the priest in a while. He's known me for most of my life. He knew Ma because she would attend his services every Sunday. He was the one who buried her.

"Donahue," I greet as I answer.

"You should get to the club. All the brothers need to be with you when I tell you where to go next. This is important, Cathal. I'll send you the address in text." His voice is calm, but there's a hint of something I can't put my finger on. I want to question him on it, but he hangs up, and then the message comes through.

My chest tightens when I open it. On the screen is the address for the house Moore told us about. I don't know why Donahue is there, why he's calling me to come to Bragan's home, but I'll get to the bottom of it.

I've always trusted Donahue. But it's only because he's been around my family all my life. The old man has never done or said anything wrong, and yet my gut churns with frustration.

Has he been hiding Bragan all this time?

I rush back to the club in record time because I'm tense. It's going to take us at least thirty minutes to get to the address Donahue sent. The moment I walk into the living room, I find five of my brothers.

"Somethin's wrong," I tell them as they all look up when I rush inside. "Donahue's called; he wants us to meet him at Bragan's place."

Rebel leans forward, intrigued. "What?"

"Aye." I nod. "I'm as confused as you are. Let's ride."

I turn and am out the door with all of them hot on my heels. I make my way to my bike and start the engine. As each of the bikes come to life, the noise is a feckin' symphony. Life on two wheels has become as natural as breathin' to me. I can't imagine ever lovin' somethin' more than being out on the open road.

With my brothers behind me, following and supporting me as they've done for all these years, I know I'm finally going to close a part of my life that's plagued me for too long. There's tension in my muscles, though. I can feel it running in my veins. The idea that the bastard could get away.

So many thoughts run through my mind when I consider having him in my grasp and then losing him again. I don't want that to happen. I need this to work out.

CHAPTER FIVE

Miren

The past few days have been tense. I've spent it with men who would make Satan fear. I didn't expect to ever be in a position where I would need to run, but with every session of torture they bestow on me, I can't help but pray for help. When the door creaks open and one of the goons who I learned is named Nolan walks in, I know I'm in for another session. It's enough to have bile rising up my throat and burning its way into my oesophagus.

All my life, I've never wanted for anything. But in

the world I now find myself being held captive, all I want is my freedom. I grew up around respectable people, honest people, but in this place, those are merely stories of fiction. Looking around me, I don't find them.

I stare at the bodyguard who watches me intently. There's a savagery in his gaze that makes me shiver. I can't imagine what he's thinking when he looks at me. The man I know to be my father doesn't show any paternal instinct, and the pain he inflicts will forever scar me. I know it will.

"C'mere to me," Nolan orders. "He's waiting on you. And he doesn't like to be late."

"Late for what?"

"Never you mind," he bites out, and I can tell he's frustrated by the way he fists his hands and his face creases when he glares at me. "Come now, *cailín*, time to go."

Go? Maybe they're releasing me. I haven't been of help to them, so perhaps they're finally letting me see Mum and we can return to London. My chest blooms with hope as I push to my feet and follow Nolan on the path that leads to a staircase. This house is built on underground tunnels. I don't know where they all go, but if I weren't afraid for my life, I'd love to explore.

When we reach the living room, the memory of only a few days ago flickers in my mind. My father returned from the garden, and as much as he tried to hide the crimson on his hands, he couldn't. Death followed him like a shadow. Blood stained his hands, and the stench of metal burned my nostrils. I can never forget that day.

An image flashed into my mind, a memory of a movie scene—a man's eyes vacant as they stared out at nothing. His mouth parted in a scream which never came—but I'm pretty sure it was a daily occurrence in Patrick Bragan's life.

There must be so many innocent lives destroyed by the man I should look up to as if he were a hero. But I've come to learn my father is far from it.

I know better than to take anyone at face value anymore. We learn from the Bible that Satan lives in hell, that he rules it, but I have come face-to-face with the Devil, and he is my father. A man who thinks that respect is forced, and he can get anything he wants. It seems the men who work for him have given him that privilege.

But I can't.

I don't want to.

I'm not a gullible little girl anymore, and he knows

it. There's no doubt this man can see my strength, but he can also see the fear he instils in me.

"There she is," he says as I enter the living room where he's seated in an armchair. The house is immaculate. You would never guess it belongs to a criminal. On movies, most times the bad guy's house is a dank, dreary building. This, however, is fit for a king. "Sit."

"What do you want from me?" I ask him as I sit, but I don't relax. I can't.

Even though he seems to be in a good mood, I can't tell if he'll suddenly turn nasty. He's certainly proven to have a short fuse. Perhaps that's where I get it from. When I was younger, mum would always tell me I need to breathe through my anger or frustration. So, I heed her advice in this moment.

"It seems yer Ma has eluded me," he says, surprising me.

Over the past few days, he questioned me about Mum's business, but I haven't been able to offer him any insight. But he hasn't truly spoken of their relationship, and he hasn't mentioned knowing where she is.

"What do you mean?"

"She's disappeared. Left you all alone. That's not what a mother should do to her child. Is it?" He's taunting me.

I can tell from the smirk on his face he knows what he's saying is hurting me. Since he took me, I've been worried about her. I was convinced he stole her, that he kidnapped her before he took me.

But it seems she made it out.

"I don't know what you mean. The last time I saw her she was at home. And then you kidnapped me, so I have no clue where she is. But she will find me."

"I truly wish she does," he informs me as he pulls a cigar from his pocket. It's thick, and even though it's not lit yet, the smell is strong as it wafts over to me.

The door opens, and more men walk in. I look over to them, and I can't help but marvel at just how big this house is. The entrance hall is enormous. Then when I look forward once more, I notice the open patio doors allow light to stream in from the back garden. Each time I've been allowed up here, I've noticed small things like windows that are open where I could possibly squeeze through and escape.

I want to leave. But I've been forced to stay within the grounds of the enormous house my father had built. He told me with pride about his home. Every brick laid was done under his watchful stare. He ensured everything was done to his liking. A man who wants to rule everything in his life. But I'm sure he realises, I'm not one of those things.

"I think you'll be very happy here," he tells me, drawing my attention back to him.

"I don't want to live here."

"You'll be known as the princess," he informs me with a smile. And for a moment, I think he's joking. He still hasn't told me who he really is. There's no way he's a businessman. He must be a criminal. A very good one when you take in the house he lives in. "You can live in a castle. This home needs a woman's touch."

"A prisoner princess in a castle built on lies and the blood of men," I throw back as anger surges through me. But my cheeky remark has him chuckling.

It will never be a home to me, only a prison that keeps me hostage.

"There's nothing I can't buy you, Miren. You can have the world if you choose."

"I don't want anything from you. There's nothing you can buy to make me love you." My voice is filled with false confidence. "I need to freshen up," I say suddenly before he can respond to my retort.

He looks at me for a long time before he gestures to one of the guards.

"Take her."

I'm dragged to my feet and led through a maze of

corridors until the man holding me shoves open a door and waits for me to enter the bathroom. Once inside, I'm alone, and I'm able to breathe. The first thing I do is check the window, but it looks like it's been locked. I can't turn the handle, which hinders me from pushing it open. Nobody should be afraid in their own home, which is why this will never be a place I can live.

"Where does the little princess think she's going?" A deep, gravelly, male voice comes from the doorway, surprising me.

His British accent is posh, and I'm shocked he's not Irish as well. Patrick, my father, hasn't told me where we are. I can tell it's the countryside, but apart from trees I've seen through the windows, I could be anywhere in the country.

"I wanted some fresh air."

He glares at me, and I know he doesn't believe me. "Come." It's only one word, but it scares me. I notice him fist his hands at his sides, and I note he has the knuckles of a fighter.

"I'm not done," I inform him, lifting my chin with an air of confidence I don't at all feel.

If any one of Patrick's men will hurt me, it's this man. He looks like he's ex-army, and I'm pretty sure he's well trained to take down mercenaries. I don't see how a twenty-two-year-old college girl would be able to fight him off.

"Miren," my father's voice calls to me from the hallway. "What's taking so long in here?" I turn to find him standing just behind the guard at the open door. The look on his face tells me I'm going to be locked in my prison cell for the unforeseeable future. There is no response that will keep him calm, so I don't reply.

He moves into the room and notices I'm right at the window. There's no denying what I was trying to do.

"I asked you a question," he seethes before making his way toward me. Each calculated step he takes sends ice racing through my veins.

"I... I wanted some fresh air," I tell him, attempting to keep my tone calm. "It's not really out of the question. Is it?"

He ponders this for a moment before he smiles. "Not at all." He turns to the door and gestures for his guard to step back. "Just remember, my men enjoy the chase. And I can't stop them from doing what they need to once they catch you." He shuts the door with the ghost of his warning gripping my chest.

I close my eyes and breathe deeply. A need to run still courses through my veins, but I don't. I know I'll be killed if I try. And knowing my mother is alive and out there somewhere, I decide to see this through.

Back in the living room, I settle on the chair I was in earlier. Patrick is on the phone. I can't bring myself to consider calling him Dad, but that's who he is.

"I don't give a fuck," he curses into the speaker. "If those bastards come near me, I will kill them all." His threat is pure venom. I wonder who he's talking about. "I'll make sure they pay." He hangs up before turning to look at me once more. "Feeling better?"

"Yes."

"Good. Now, we're going to take a little trip. Get away for a while. I'd like to show you what a luxurious life you'll have if you agree to stay here." He offers me a grin that seems genuine, but the man is a savage.

"Why? I know what you do. It's not like you can hide it. You hurt people for fun," I throw back and immediately regret it because the look my father gives me is pure venom. "I'm sorry. I just... I want to go home." I've never been able to lie to my mother, and now I realise I can't lie to the man who has stolen me either.

"You think you know me, wee one?" he says with a chuckle. "You have no fucking clue who we are. The blood that runs through yer veins is filled with violence. From before yer great-grandfather was the leader of the Irish mob. He was born in Ireland, he married and had one son and one daughter who he knew would be able to take over the mob he ran with an iron fist."

"You're..." My mouth drops open as I consider the repercussions of his words. My family are part of the mob. They're *the* mob. Fuck.

"Now, we're going to head out—"

"Boss," one of the men comes rushing in. "The perimeter has been breached."

Patrick looks directly at me. "You will go up to the bedroom with Declan and stay there until I call you down," he orders before spinning on his heel and racing from the living room with the rest of the guards. My father heads for the opposite side of the entrance hall, and the door is shut on his actions.

Declan brings me to the room I woke up in a few days ago and leaves me inside. He shuts the door, but I listen for a click of the lock, which never comes. In the bedroom, I open the balcony doors and step out. I can hear a young guy speaking, "I'm not fucking telling you anything," he spits, and I am surprised. I doubt anyone would talk to Patrick like that and live. I'm pretty sure most would beg for their lives.

"You'll tell me all about those Royal Bastards. The MC will be taken down, whether you help me or not."

Patrick's tone is filled with rage. A motorcycle club. It's the only thing I can think of when I overhear him say *MC*.

I've heard mention of a few motorcycle clubs before. But it was only one late night not long after I got here that I heard some of the guards whisper about the President who's out for blood. They spoke of him as if he were the Devil. And I wondered if he's as bad as they think. Then one of them mentioned his methods of torture, and that's when I realised I thought my father was a monster, but the rumours about Cathal, the biker, are far worse.

I hear more cars arriving as the gravel under the tires crunch.

"Father Donahue," Dad's voice calls to the man stepping out of the car. "What are you doing here?"

"Things are heating up in Belfast," the older man says, and there's no doubt in my mind he's talking to my father. "You need to give up this witch hunt before someone gets hurt. She's gone, and she's not coming back. It's time you cleaned up this organisation."

"I will never give up." There's conviction in my father's voice.

"They've sent me to talk some sense into you. Please, Patrick, there are better ways. You know she's stronger than you in this," Father Donahue says, the worry evident in his tone. I'm not sure exactly who the *they* or *she* are, but I can only assume it's the motorcycle club. It's the only thing I can think of.

My father laughs out loud at the priest's warning. "They can try. Nobody touches me or my daughter." I'm surprised by his words. My father mentioned me. I'm the only family he has it seems. But then again, he could so easily be talking about the mob.

"Where is Miren?" Father Donahue asks then, and that only shocks me further. I didn't think the man would know me since I've never met him.

"In her room. She won't come out here until I call to her. I don't need her witnessing anything untoward." His tone is confident. There's an edge to his voice which tells me he doesn't want to be argued with, not about this.

"I'll go up and see her," the older man says, and then all I hear are the crunching footfalls of his shoes. I wonder what would happen if I were to try and escape now. I'm pretty sure Declan is downstairs. If I could slip out of the bedroom and try the window in another room, perhaps I can climb down somehow. This balcony doesn't offer any assistance since it leads right down to the front of the house.

In the distance, I can hear the rumble of more engines, but this time, not cars. No, these are deep, vibrating rumbles. They're motorbikes. As they near, I turn to find Father Donahue at the door of my bedroom.

"Miren," he says my name with reverence. "It's so lovely to meet you. I'm Father Donahue. I've known yer parents for a long while." He offers me a kind smile, and I relax.

"It's nice to meet you too. My mother has never mentioned you." My words seem to have an effect on the older man. There's a sadness in his gaze, and then he nods.

"I'm sorry it has come to this, Miren." Guilt flickers in his gaze for a short moment, and then it's as if the world tilts on its axis. An explosion from below the house shakes the walls, and the floor of my bedroom seems to vibrate with it. Windows shatter, and I'm on the floor, crawling to the exit as the priest races for me. He pulls me to my feet, and we rush from the crumbling home I was kept a prisoner in. Another eruption comes from the ground floor, and as we exit through the front door, I'm slammed to the ground. Just outside the house, the heat of the fire warms me, and when I glance over my shoulder, I notice how it wreaks havoc on the house I considered a cage. We crawl away, needing to escape.

I glance back to see the walls come down.

"Say nothing," Father Donahue hisses at me as he drags me to my feet, and we run as fast as we can and as far away from the house as possible until we collapse on the grass. "Say nothing about who you are," he tells me. "Do you hear me, girl?"

"What?" Confusion clouds my mind, and I'm not sure what he's talking about.

"When I introduce ye, ye will say nothing about being a Bragan or who yer da is. You are a new woman from this day forward." He stands, then offers me a hand. Blood drips from his wrinkled flesh, and I realise he's hurt himself.

I take his proffered hand, and he pulls me up. "But—"

The old man glances over his shoulder, and that's when I notice the myriad of chrome and leather. He looks to me again. "Yer name is Miren Doyle."

"But—" I don't have time to say anything more, because the moment I open my mouth, the heavy footsteps interrupt me. And Father Donahue's eyes widen when he looks behind me. As I turn, I find a man who looks like he can crush me with one hand staring back at us.

He's tall. His broad shoulders are strong under the white T-shirt and the leather cut. Dark eyes land on me for a second, then he lifts them to the priest behind me. And I'm not ready for the voice that comes from his perfectly full lips.

"Donahue," he greets the priest.

CHAPTER SIX

Monster

The closer we get to the house, the more my muscles tense. My hands grip the bars tighter with every mile. Soon, I'll come face-to-face with the bastard who killed my mother. I smile when I take the last corner, but it falls when I see the destruction before me. I didn't expect to see the house in tatters. Some of the windows have blown out, and the second floor reminds me of the ruins of a castle.

There are sirens in the distance, and I know without a doubt, there won't be much privacy when the peelers arrive. I spot Donahue standin' with a young girl. Or woman. At least, that's what I think when she tilts her head towards him.

Her long, dark hair hangs to just above her arse. I can't help but notice the curve of her jeans is rounded perfectly. Feck. I'm getting distracted. Killing the engine, I head over to where they're stood and force myself not to look at the pretty young thing.

"Donahue," I greet the man I've known all my life. I should be focused on askin' him about what happened, but the wee girl that's stood beside him has captured my attention. At first, I thought it was Bragan's daughter, but I don't know if he had any wee ones. If he did, he kept them well hidden. But this girl with her chocolate brown hair and blue-grey eyes can't be the daughter of the mob boss. At least, that's what I try to convince myself of as I close the distance between us. "Who's this?"

"Miren Doyle. She was captured by Bragan for questioning." His words send ice through my veins. The girl has dried scars on her shoulder and arms. Her lip is swollen on the left, and her one eye has a bruise just below it.

"What happened here?" I look away from the girl because, even under all the scars and bruising, she's gorgeous. I can't deny it.

"Two explosions went off," Donahue tells me. "Your man is inside." We turn to look at the wreckage, and I know there's no way he's going to walk out of there. I told Scout not to do it, but the wee bastard didn't listen to me. I don't like losing men, and because he was only a prospect, my gut churns with anger and frustration.

He wanted to prove himself to me, but all he did was get himself killed. "Where is Bragan?" I ask, keeping my eyes on the brothers pulling the mob's soldiers from the rubble. "I want him."

"He's dead," Donahue tells me, which causes me to look over at the old man. "He went into the basement with Scout and the rest of his guards."

From what I can see, I doubt anyone who was under the house is coming out with all their limbs attached, let alone breathing. I wanted so much to kill the bastard who shot my mother. Revenge isn't complete until I have his blood on my hands. But it seems fate, the fickle bitch, has taken that from me.

"I want to see the body," I tell Donahue before leaving him with the girl. I don't know who she is, and I don't particularly care right now.

I make my way to the crumbling house and find

Rebel and Rogue carrying out remains on a stretcher. The van we brought, which drove behind all the bikes, is parked up closer now, and as they take the charred pieces of whoever the feck they're carrying to the vehicle, I take in the property.

I wanted to find closure on my own. It's been taken away from me, just like my ma was all those years ago. Rebel steps up beside me and watches the men working. With the firemen doing their job getting the blaze under control, I wonder briefly if this was all planned. There's no body, and I know Bragan is a feckin' arsehole when it comes to escaping. I've heard the rumours of him evading death numerous times.

"I don't like this," I tell Rebel without looking at my VP.

I can feel Rebel's stare on me. "You think he escaped before the explosions?" I nod, and he continues. "Then we'll find the fecker. We did it once. we will do it again."

"If he's alive." Saviour walks up to us and hands me a small memento from the rubble. A gold Rolex that, when I turn it over, bears the inscription — Loyalty or Death — and below it are the initials — *P.B.* — Patrick Bragan.

"C-Can I leave now?" A soft voice comes from behind me, and I can't deny hearing it makes my cock ache. It's been a while since I've allowed myself the pleasure of a woman. Perhaps that's why, when I turn around, I find myself staring at the girl who was with Donahue.

The priest looks at me, his eyes locked on mine, and I can tell he's wanting to ask me something. And I've a feelin' that what he's about to ask me I won't like one bit.

"What?"

"I was wondering if Miren here can stay with you at the clubhouse for a short time. She needs protectin' because Bragan's men will be comin' after her. She knows too much. Now that he's dead…"

He allows his words to trail off, and I can't deny the old bastard is good. He wants to play on my empathy, and as I look at him, I know there's no way to refuse his request.

I run the club with an iron fist. My vow is not to allow innocents to get hurt. I want Ma to be proud of me, for the most part, as she looks down from heaven. Even if I don't believe in it, I know she did. So, in my mind, I *see* her up there.

"Aye," I say with a nod. "She can stay, but nothin' comes for free," I tell the old man as I glance at the pretty girl.

From head to toe, she looks like a feckin' temptress. The brothers are going to try their luck with her, I can see it now. But even as I think it, an unknown emotion twists in my gut. I don't like it.

I'm going to have to tell them they're not allowed to touch. I've done it before, but never because of jealousy. For a long moment, I take her in. She is stunnin'. A classic beauty with flowing dark hair and full pink lips that look like they shimmer. Her eyes, though, they capture me for too feckin' long. The colour changing between blue and silver. It's as if they're magic.

"You know how to clean?" I ask her, keeping my voice low, filled with anger and frustration.

She nods. "Yes, I can. I'm happy to do any job you have for me."

Her words may be innocent, but the thoughts runnin' through my mind are far from it. Feck. I can't afford to get distracted. But she could hold a fountain of information on Bragan. And that's one of the main reasons I'm agreein' to this stupid feckin' idea.

"Right then," I tell her before glancing at Rebel. "Take her in the van. Find an empty room and set her up. I'll be back shortly."

"Aye, will do." He gestures with his head, and the pretty girl follows him to the van.

"Thank you," Donahue says to me. "She's a good girl, just needs to find her feet. I'm sure she won't be a bother for too long."

"She won't be. I don't keep strays," I inform him. "You say she was kidnapped by Bragan?"

He nods. "I don't know the extent of it. But I arrived today to talk to him, having overheard there was a girl here," he tells me, and I know if I were to ask about where he heard the news from, he won't tell me. Any confessions made to a priest are meant to be confidential. I can't ask him to break his vow.

"She must be someone important if he wanted her here." My remark has him nodding slowly. "You know I ain't goin' ta go easy on her. I want information, and if she's been in that house," I say as I gesture towards what's now a disaster zone, "she will be questioned."

The peelers pull up with sirens blaring. I expected them sooner, but it seems the feckers are late. I never once thought I'd come to need them, but they're on the payroll, and they need to keep me informed just as much as I do them. They turn a blind eye to some of our operations, which I'm thankful for. I don't need these feckers breathin' down my neck when I'm tryin' to make money for the club.

Sergeant O'Malley saunters up to where we're

standing and removes his helmet. The fact that he owns a Harley makes him slightly less of a twat than the rest of his force.

"You have anything to do with this, O'Connor?" he asks as he looks over the scene while using my last name. None of the brothers acknowledge the name. Not because they don't respect me, but when Ma died, I let it go. I became Monster, and that's the only version of me they've come to know. And I wouldn't have it any other way. There is no longer Cathal O'Connor. He died along with the woman who reared him.

"Aye, can ye see I'm standin' here with the feckin' bomb in my hand?"

"Part of my job to ask," he tells me, and Donahue chuckles. "Father."

Donahue utters solemnly, "There's only one man responsible for his own demise, and it's Bragan himself. This was premeditated, I'm sure."

"What makes you say that?" I question, glancing at the old man.

Donahue stares off into the distance, and I wonder if the man is hiding truths. I don't trust many. It doesn't matter if they're a man of God or not. I've learned over the years that no vow is too sacred to stop someone from lying.

"A man like him didn't do things for no reason," the priest says. "Everything is planned; there aren't any situations left to chance. Especially one like this."

"Pres," Racer calls to me as he closes the distance. "There's nothing else on the site."

Racer's been my Road Captain for a couple of years now. As soon as he patched in, I knew he would be the one to take over the position. He has a good head on his shoulders, but he's also focused. He's a good lad.

"Grand," I tell him. "Meet you back at the compound. And tell everyone church will start in thirty."

We'll need to sit down and figure this shite out. I can't have people thinkin' we were responsible for this blast. And we also need to keep the peace with Dublin. I know Bragan had a wife who ran off across the pond. It means I'll have to contact Jameson and see if he has any contacts over there who might know somethin'.

Once the brothers have left, I turn to Donahue. "Find her a place. I don't want her in my home for longer than I need to."

"Cathal—"

"It's Monster," I interrupt him. Anger at the fact he's here, at the house of the man I want dead, courses through me. "Did you know he was here all this time?" It's no secret to him I believed Bragan killed Ma. I made it very clear what I wanted, and who I wanted. "Because if you did," I say, pausing for a moment before I continue, "I will end you. Make no mistake about that."

Without another word, I saunter off to my bike. I leave the priest and sergeant at the site while I pull out onto the road.

I'm still unsure of what to do about the girl. She's going to cause shite within the club, and I don't like it. My men may be loyal, but women are serpents. They'll lure you in until you have no other choice but to give them what they ask for.

The rumble of my engine is the only thing that calms me down. I consider what Ma would say about the girl. She always believed I would find love. Even though I didn't. Relationships distract. I don't need that in my life. My brothers mean more to me than a woman. There was only one person I loved, and it was my mother.

I didn't even love my father, which says something about the man he was. I looked up to him in certain respects, but as a man, he was a bastard. The road is busy as I weave through traffic heading west. Our clubhouse is just outside the main city centre. A place we can be ourselves.

When I pull up to the clubhouse, I offer a nod of greeting to the prospects who are busy cleaning a couple of the brothers' bikes. Killing the engine, I head inside to find the bar already packed. Some of the brothers sit with their old ladies, while those who are single have some of the club whores on their laps.

"Church," I call out as I stalk through the bar. I don't stop for a drink, but I do notice the new girl sitting with Callia. I can feel her stare, her gaze on me, as I make my way to the back of the building and walk through the doors. There's no need for me to notice her, to look at her, but I can't help my glance from darting her way before the rest of the men enter.

She's watching me. The moment my gaze lands on her, though, she looks away. This is going to be a problem. Each of the brothers take their seats. It's good to see all the brothers here, safe. With the shite we're having to deal with, I need their support. Their focus.

Once everyone has set their phones in the box, Tye, who is our resident Tech, takes it and sets it outside the meeting room. No phones allowed while we're in here. It's more a security measure than anything else. Also, I need the men focused.

We're all settled before I start. "We all know about the explosion at the Bragan compound. I'm not convinced the bastard is dead," I tell them. "Tye, I want you looking into every possible contact this fecker has. Also, let's dig into his wife. Find out where she is and let me know. Jameson is always willin' to help, and I think we're going to need him in on this."

"No problem." Tye nods with a grin. "I'll have info for you before dinner," he tells me easily. He's good at what he does. Even though he's a youngen, I trust his expertise. I've watched him hack into the Garda's network far too many times, and every time, I'm impressed.

"There are places a man like him can go," I say before looking at every man in the room. Each of them brothers. Family. They may not be blood, but I trust them more than I would anyone else in my life.

We have been through some shite together. Each time I had a lead on who killed my mother, on finding Bragan, my brothers would be there for me. After he murdered my ma, the bastard didn't stay in Ireland, not for long anyway, that's for sure.

The property he ended up in may have been close by, but the mob have so many properties to hide their soldiers. We had no idea where he was, and as the leader, he was able to stay underground and never get his hands dirty. A man like him would hire people for that shite.

"Pres," Sully says. "I cleaned up the warehouse. Found this on the body." He pushes a metal clasp—with a shimmering emerald on the front—along the table, and it slides down to where I'm sat. I pick it up and find it looks expensive. It could be his wife's.

"Find out if the arsehole had any family, kids." I didn't even think about the outcome before I killed him. They'd be better off without him anyway. At least, that's what I tell myself.

No child should grow up in that life. They shouldn't know violence.

I know it can't be stopped, but if there ever was an option to save a youngen from being brought up around violence, I'd do it.

"Look into this," I tell Rebel as I hand him the sparkly object. "I'm going to get on the phone to Jameson in New Orleans. Feckin' time difference will put it at about midday over there, I reckon. Once his men find Bragan's wife, we'll have to either fly over or bring the *cailín* over here. One way or another, we will speak to her, and we'll get answers. If Bragan is still alive, she's the first person he'll go to."

"How do ye know?" This comes from Brute. That's his road name. The fecker's real name is Hades. And at times, I wonder if the bastard has come from hell itself.

"If ye were hidin' out, ye'd go to the one person who would lie for ye." I shake my head. "Doesn't matter if they're no together anymore. Safety's what matters. And I've a feeling she'll take the criminal in."

"We also need to find out about any kin," Racer suggests, and I nod again. He's right.

"Aye," I say, then look back at Tye. "Can you dig into the records and find out if they had any wee ones?"

"Will do."

"Anythin' else I missed?" I look at each brother, face-to-face. None of them offer up anythin' more, which means the meetin' is over. "That's it," I say, hitting the gavel on the smooth wooden surface. "Let's drink."

CHAPTER SEVEN

Miren

I try not to look at him, but my eyes seem to be like magnets, and he's the metal. I'm in his home, a place where I'm surrounded by danger, because if they found out who I really am, they'll kill me. There's no doubt in my mind I'm the enemy. As he watched them carry body parts from the wreckage, I could tell from the anger in his expression he wanted those to be of my father.

I don't know who he is, or why he hates us, but I plan to find out. I glance at Callia who's sipping her beer and smile. "So," I start. "How long have you been living with the club?"

She shrugs. "A couple of years now. They found me on the streets, turning tricks. Racer over there," she says gesturing towards the guy with ink all the way up his arms to his neck. His dark hair stands in spikes, and his deep blue eyes are on the girl sitting in his lap. "He came across me when I was out in Dublin. He was on a run and wanted to hire me. When he found out I wasn't old enough to be doing that shite, he lost his mind."

"How old were you?"

"Sixteen," she informs me with a wink. "I had to grow up pretty fast, and when I ran away from home, I didn't plan on going back. So, I did what I needed to."

She doesn't seem at all perturbed at telling me this, but I'm shocked anyone at that age would even consider selling themselves.

But then again, I've been lucky all my life.

Even though my mother was focused on her work, she ensured I was safe and looked after. I never needed for anything. Some would say I was spoiled, but I didn't see it that way. With the schooling and the gifts I received, they never could equal the love of a parent. My mother was good in setting rules and boundaries, but she never offered me the gentle affection most maternal figures do.

"That's… that's so sad," I finally say to Callia.

When I was brought here a few hours ago, I was given one of the bedrooms upstairs and introduced to her. Out of all the women here, she's closest to my age and not one of the club whores as she calls them.

"I'm okay now," she tells me happily. "Life happens when you're planning yer future. I'm lucky Monster took me in. He's a good man." I follow her eye line and find the President of the MC looking directly at us. Callia offers him a wave, which he responds to with a nod. "He's so hot," she whispers now, and I can't help but want to agree with her. But I don't. Not that I don't think he is, but I know men like him. They're dangerous; they'll kill without thinking, and something tells me Monster wants me dead.

"I guess." It's all I can add to my new friend's comment.

She giggles and turns to me. "You ever had a boyfriend, lassie?"

I think about the guys who I've been on dates with and shake my head. "Not really. I wasn't really allowed to date. My mother would have killed me and whoever the guy was. There was one, just before I graduated, but..." I catch myself before I can speak out of turn. I can't tell her I had a boyfriend just before I was kidnapped by my father.

"What?"

"I just haven't had *that* much experience with lads, especially ones much older than I am." I shrug it off, but as I say this, my thoughts stray to Monster.

"You're a virgin?" she whispers, her eyes wide.

"Not exactly," I say. "I've done it a couple of times, but..."

Leaning closer to ensure nobody around us can hear her, a soft giggle falls from her lips. "Which means you're practically a virgin."

"Not practically," I retort while my cheeks heat. "I know how it all works." This has us laughing out loud, and I feel Monster's gaze on us. As much as I can't stop looking at him, it seems the man can't tear his eyes away from me. "Anyway," I say. "You were one once as well; so, it's not that far-fetched to think about. Is it?"

Callia smiles, then shrugs. "Aye, you're right, but you're a year older than me, so it's odd to me. Nothing wrong with it," she continues, nudging me with her shoulder.

"I guess now I'm away from home, I'm going to have to figure out what to do with my life." I'm not really talking to her. The thought spills from my mouth before I have time to consider it.

"You could work at the club," she tells me easily. "I'm there five nights a week. It's good pay, and you're able to save up. Soon, I'll be out of here. But I'll never forget what the MC has done for me."

This captures my attention. "The club?"

"Aye, the boys run a bar and strip club closer to town. It's safe, and the girls are looked after. You don't have to take yer clothes off. There are other things to do. I waitress. There is no touching, but if you give them a smile, the feckers leave good tips. You can save, and then you'll be able to find your freedom again."

Her voice echoes my thoughts.

Freedom.

I have never known what that feels like. It's always been me against Mum's rules. On one hand, I know she was trying to keep me safe, but on the other, I realise how much of a prison my life had become.

Going back to London and picking up my old life isn't going to be possible. The men will always be hunting me down. I will have a target on my back.

"I'll think about it," I tell her, but I know I may not have a choice.

The thing about it is, I can't afford to tell them who

I am. I don't know if my father really did die in that explosion. He may be hiding out. If he is, I'm still in danger.

And if he is alive, he will come for me.

"Lia," one of the other girls calls, "Are we heading to the city?"

The brunette walks up to us, her eyes never straying towards me. It's as if she doesn't notice I'm even here. I've become used to people trying to avoid me, but this is different. I'm out of my depth. These girls know each other, they're all friends. I'm an outsider who should find her own way.

I hop off the stool and offer a smile at Callia. She's been nice to me, and I don't want to be rude. "I need fresh air."

I leave her with her friend and make my way outside. The night is dark, with only the full moon offering illumination. The compound we're on is large, but there isn't a lot of lighting. I move away from the house, my mind focused on my future. The unknown is scary.

The music from the bar filters through to the outside where I'm standing. Closing my eyes, I listen to the lyrics from 'How to Save a Life' and wonder if I'll be able to stay alive and leave here before Monster finds out who I really am. "I hope so," I whisper to myself.

"You do?" A deep voice startles me, and I spin on my heel to find the man in question.

Monster's tall. I'm only five four, and yet, I only reach his chest. His broad shoulders seem to strain against his white tee, and the cut he's wearing completes the look of a dangerous villain.

"Sorry, I was just..." I don't know what to say to him. There's nothing I can say that won't get me into trouble, nothing true anyway. I hate lying. My mother did it to me, for years, and I've never wanted to keep secrets from anyone. However, here I find myself doing it without flinching.

"Just?" He crosses his arms over his chest, which only makes him seem larger than life. The air between us is electric. As if he's charged it with whatever is hidden inside him. He isn't a man—he's more monster than anything else. He belongs in the shadows, in the darkness.

"Thinking out loud." I finally decide on my response, but it won't appease the man before me. He doesn't trust me, and I don't trust him either. We've come to an impasse, and nothing is going to change that.

"Who are you, little girl?"

"I'm not a little girl for one," I tell him. "I'm twenty-two." I don't know why I feel the need to defend myself to him, but I can't stop myself.

The corner of his mouth tilts as he regards me.

"Why did Bragan want to question ye?" he asks as he pulls out a packet of smokes and taps one out. I watch as he presses it between his full lips and lights it up. The red cherry burns as Monster inhales a lungful of smoke.

"I don't know."

"You don't?" He arches a dark brow at me. In the silver light of the moon, he looms over me, his shadow cocooning me from the outside world. "I think ye're lyin' to me. Unless ye're hidin' somethin' else. Maybe ye're his kin…"

"I am nothing to him," I spit out, and I'm surprised at how adamant I am at denouncing my father. Even though he's evil, he's still my blood.

"Fair enough." Monster nods. "I take it ye don't have any family?"

I don't look at him; instead, I focus on the garden. It's pretty out here. Not far from the city, but far enough that you don't have traffic or people randomly walking by. It's a nice piece of land. Somewhere I could have called home if I were staying.

"No," I tell him finally. "I don't."

My heart thunders in my chest when Monster reaches for my chin, his index finger tipping my head towards him. "Then you'll find a place here."

"I'm not staying."

This time, he steps in front of me, right up against me. He's in my personal space, and yet I don't fight him. This close, I truly take in the face before me. He's handsome, annoyingly so. I don't want to find him attractive, but I would be blind if I said he isn't. He's breathtakingly gorgeous. Which is a problem, and one of the reasons I can't stay here. The other reason is that he would kill me the moment he learns who I really am.

"You're not leaving. I promised Donahue I would keep you safe until he finds you a new home. A new job."

"I can't stay—"

"If ye walk out those gates, Bragan's men will come for ye. They'll kill ye," Monster tells me quickly.

I can't fight him on it because I know it's true. They will find me. My father's men were experts at their jobs. And now he's gone, I'm nothing to them. I have insider knowledge about who they are and what they've done for him. I'm a threat.

"Well, I can't stay here. I'm not...I'm not part of your

club."

"The lassies who come here need protection. We offer that." He drops the smoke and crushes it with his heavy, black boot. The gravel crunches underfoot with the movement, and then Monster glances up at me. "I don't trust anyone I don't know. But I won't let a wee *cailín* out in the world, knowing she could be hurt."

I don't know why his words send warmth through me, but they do. I've always been hidden away from others. I was raised in a world without men like him—dangerous, rugged, and ultimately handsome. No guys were allowed near me, not until Mum finally acquiesced and first permitted me to date a year ago.

"Trust should be earned," I tell him, tipping my chin up. "I know you don't know me, and I don't expect you to trust me, which is why I thought leaving would be easier than having you put up with some stranger in your home."

Monster stares at me for a long while, and for a moment, I wonder if he can see more of my father in my eyes.

Does he recognise the cold, calculated stare Patrick had?

He finally nods. "You'll stay."

He doesn't leave it open to debate because he steps back and turns on his heel, leaving me in the darkness.

I watch him walk back into the bar, and for a moment, I miss him. Just a second of need courses through me. I've never truly wanted someone to be near me. But with him, I wasn't at all scared. The fear of him hurting me wasn't there. It was the anxiety of him finding out who I am and sending me away that frightened me.

Even though I've made the decision to leave, I glance back at the clubhouse, and I wonder what it would be like to be wanted, needed, to be cared for, rather than to be treated like a second thought.

"Hey, precious," a deep voice comes from the shadows. All I can see is the cherry of the smoke from whoever it is. "Monster seems to be intrigued by you." When the stranger steps out of the darkness, I take him in.

He's tall, with slightly long black hair that hits his shoulders. His tanned skin is evidence he spends a lot of time outside. Almost sun-kissed, even up here in the North. But it's his eyes that steal my breath. They're golden, almost as if they're shimmering in the darkness.

"Who are you?" I turn to regard him.

Crossing my arms, I hug myself, hoping I can hold myself together as this man assesses me.

He drops the smoke and kills it with his boot before he says, "I'm the Rev." His voice is deep, a drawl of North Irish accent along with the huskiness of a smoker. "Name's Hadrian, but everyone calls me Rev or Reverend."

"So you're like the priest of the club?" I don't know how the monikers work, if they're meaningful to what the men do, or if it's just because they felt the need for them.

Hadrian chuckles. "Aye," he answers me. "You could come to me and pray. I quite like a pretty girl on her knees asking for repentance." He steps towards me, but he doesn't reach for me. His hands remain at his sides. There's no doubt about what he means. And it's no saintly act.

"I don't believe in God," I tell him.

This intrigues him because his head tips to the side, and his eyes narrow as he watches me. "Why's that?"

"He's never been there for me," I admit as I recall the times I prayed for answers about who my father was. I wanted a family, like my friends had, but I never got it. The answers I would seek never came.

"Doors close on us all the time, precious," he tells me. "It ain't because he's not answerin'. It's because it wasn't meant for you."

"What you're telling me is that I wasn't meant to have a father?" I throw back in anger.

The idea of my father leaving before I even got a chance to know him still hurts. It's as if Hadrian has kicked me in the gut.

"I ain't sayin' that, precious. What people do to you is their choice. But how you react to it, that's on you. You can look at yer da leavin' as a bad thing, but would you be as strong and feisty if he didn't leave?"

I've spent my life angry at my mother, at my non-existent father, and the family I never had. I blamed Mum for walking out on my father, and I didn't know the reasons why she did it, because she never trusted me enough to tell me.

But, in the end, I'm an adult now, and I should let go of the sad, heartbroken girl. I doubt I could ever find it in my heart to forgive either of them for what they did to me. But Hadrian is right, I could choose to look at it in a positive light. I learned what not to do one day if I ever have children of my own.

"Thank you," I tell him.

He offers me a smile, and I'm surprised at how young he looks when he does. "That's what I'm here for, precious."

"What did you mean earlier when you said Monster is intrigued by me?"

He shakes his head slowly, lowering his gaze to the

ground between us. "I ain't seen him in such a mood in a long time. You've come in here and fecked with his plans. He's not someone who gets attached, so when he tells all the brothers to steer clear of you, I know something is up."

"He said that?" This time the shock is evident in my tone, which has Hadrian laughing out loud. "Hadrian, tell me."

He places a hand on my shoulder and gives it a little squeeze. It's an affectionate touch, but there's nothing leery about it. "You'll soon find out, precious. And call me Rev."

With that, he leaves me to ponder what he said, and I know I won't be able to get it out of my mind. Not for a long while.

CHAPTER EIGHT

Monster

Tye saunters into my office and sets down some printed pages. "This is all I could find on Bragan's wife. The rest of his files are locked up tight. I'm running some code to hack into those records, but it could take time. I wanted to get you these so you can call Jameson."

I scan the information. There isn't an address, but there is proof Sinéad landed in America a few days ago, not far from New Orleans. She's changed her name though. The strange thing is, her passport wasn't in the name of Sinéad Bragan, it was Amanda Walsh. I'm going to need help from the other chapter in the States.

I glance up at Tye. "Any children? "

"Not sure yet. If she did give birth, there isn't any proof. There should be more records somewhere. A doctor, someone. I'm tryin' to get into those. I will, ye know."

"Aye, I have no doubt ye will." It's the truth. I've seen him get into online spaces nobody would. It's why I patched him in as Tech. He's brilliant at what he does, and I'm lucky to have him.

"Everyone is out there," Tye says then. "You coming?"

"Aye, I'll be there in a few," I tell him, and I'm thankful when he doesn't press.

What's bothering me more right now, though, is the girl out there. I pick up my phone and hit dial on Donahue's number. Padraig has to give me some answers. I don't like that he's told me to toe the line and take this wee girl into my home. I don't know her.

I listen for a few rings, and when he doesn't answer, I sigh and hang up. I try Jameson. He should pick up since it's the middle of the day over the waters.

"The man they call Monster," he greets, and I can hear the smile on his face. I've known him for a wee while now, and I can safely say, he's a goodun.

"Aye, how's things wit ye?"

"Not too bad," he tells me. "What can I do for you? I have a feeling you're not just calling to check how I'm doing." He cuts to the chase, which I like. There's no faffing about.

"I'm looking for information on an Amanda Walsh. We believe her husband is the leader of the Irish mob." Even as I say it, my muscles are tight. The frustration that we didn't get the bastard is still weighing on me.

"Shit," Jameson says. "I can get Hoax to look into it for you. He'll be able to do some digging online. There will be records." The man is a legend.

"I appreciate that."

"Does this have to do with your mother?"

When I first took over the club from Da, it was Jameson who offered support and guidance. None of the men wanted me to take over. They didn't see me as leader yet, but with Jameson's advice, I was finally able to step up, to show the brothers I could do this.

"Aye." It's all I can say because each time I think of her, those feckin' feelin's I'd been hiding twist themselves in my gut. I don't like it. "When you have somethin' for me, give me a shout."

"Will do," he says before hanging up, and I settle

back in my chair.

I don't know when I'll be able to close this chapter of my life. Revenge is all I've ever known, and yet, I find comfort in it. A man's focus is as good as his goals in life. This was my only one. It had become the one thing I could hold onto. I don't know what to do without it.

I try Donahue again, but there still isn't any answer. Deep down, I wonder if something's wrong. If he's been in bed with Bragan all this time and he didn't tell me, I'm not going to be happy. Perhaps he's avoiding me. Maybe he's hiding because he doesn't want to tell me he knew where the bastard was all these years.

There's a knock on my office door, which takes my attention from the phone and Donahue to the girl standing on the threshold. I've known Callia since she was a wee one. Rebel brought her to the club after finding her in an alleyway. Life wasn't easy for her, and when she ran away from home, she didn't want to return. We took her in, and she's been here ever since. That was five years ago.

"Bout ye?" I greet as I look at her.

"Pres," she says with a smile. The soft waves of gold that is her hair fall over her face like a curtain. She's always been shy around me, but I know she sees me as an older brother. Someone who will protect her, but also, I think I scare her. Those pretty eyes though, are all for Rebel. He doesn't see it, not yet anyway. "I wanted to talk to ye bout the new girl."

"Aye?"

She nods, and I motion for her to come in. Once she's seated, she looks at me, her hands twisting in her lap. "She seems nice enough," Callia starts. "I was wonderin' if it would be nice for her to work at O'Hagans?"

I didn't think Miren would be here longer than a week at most. I wanted Donahue to find the strange girl a home, a place to go that isn't at the club. Perhaps it's my own perception of her. There's a glint in her eye I can't quite place, and reading people is my thing. I observe, with her, it's different. I can't look away, but at the same time, I hate that I *want* to look at her.

"Is this somethin' she's asked about?" I look at Callia, and I can see every pain and heartbreak she's suffered. With Miren, there's nothing. "I don't want a stranger in my home who's hidin' shite."

Callia has known me for years. She knows I don't take things lightly, and she's seen me lose myself to violence. When we learned about her, I went along with Rebel to bring her here, and that's the first time I got my hands dirty in front of one of our girls.

"She seems a nice lassie," Callia tells me. "I believe

everyone should be given a chance. I don't know her story yet, but..." The girl shakes her head, and her blonde hair swishes. "I just have a feeling she doesn't have anyone else."

The plea in her eyes twists at my chest. I couldn't say no to a pretty woman. I may not have been in love before, or ever wanted to be, but women have always been a weakness. The girls who live at the club are family, and Callia is like a wee sister to me.

"Ye reckon she's sound?" I lean back in my chair as I stare at Callia.

"Aye," she says with a nod, excitement glinting in her eyes.

I'm not entirely sure this is a good idea. But, if Miren does stay, it means I can keep an eye on her. I can find out who the feck she is and where it is she's come from. Donahue didn't just send some random girl to me.

"Tomorrow night then," I finally say. "Bring her to the club and walk her around. I don't want any shite," I warn with a pointed finger at Callia. "No arguments. She will sit back and watch what you do. I don't want her on the stage." The order is clear. Only those women I approve can take off their clothes. Reason being is, I need to know there won't be any shite in my club.

The clientele aren't scum. However, there have

been instances where boyfriends and husbands have followed along, which only ended up turning into a brawl. I can't have that happening ever again.

"Thank you," Callia says with an excited clap of her hands. "I'll take her through everything tomorrow. I just think she'll benefit from having a job, something to focus on."

"Aye." Makes sense. Even though givin' her a job will mean she'll stay here longer. Perhaps we can find her family. The thought process brings me back to Donahue. Something isn't sittin' right with me. "Tell Rebel I'm headin' out."

I push to my feet, and Callia nods. I notice the blush on her cheeks when I mention his name, and I wonder why the feck he's not made his move on her. I doubt she'll be leavin' us anytime soon. Maybe I should sit the eejit down and tell him to sort his shite out.

"I'll let him know," Callia says before leaving me to gather my things. Shrugging on my cut, I make my way out through the back of the house. I don't want to be dragged into the partying brothers right now. I need to talk to Donahue, get his thoughts on this girl.

Gettin' Tye to dig into her past may be an option, but first, I'll talk to the priest. He'll have to give me answers. The moment I reach the bikes, I spot someone in the garden. The side of the house overlooks acres of land that goes on for miles before the perimeter. It's one of the reasons Da wanted to have security cameras installed around the fence. It took a few days, but we're safe here. It's our haven.

I make my way to the shadowed figure and find it's Miren. She's not heard me approach. Her focus is on the sky. There aren't many stars out, but the moon illuminates her as she looks up at it. I wonder if she's praying to God.

I'm quiet for a long while as I watch her. Even though I can't bring myself to look away, I know I can't trust her. Not until I know who she really is. As much as I want to be a good person, to take her in and keep her safe, like I've done with all the other women who needed help, something about Miren doesn't sit right with me.

I turn and take a step towards my bike when I hear her. "Where are you going?"

I glance over my shoulder to find her looking at me. "Donahue isn't answerin' his phone," I tell her. "I'm goin' ta have a chat with him."

"May I go with you?"

She walks up to me, no fear in her eyes, which has me on alert. Most girls see me and there's a hint of fear that shimmers in their gazes. I'm tall, broad, and a scary fecker. But Miren doesn't seem at all perturbed by me.

"No."

"Please? He helped me when he found me at Patrick's house. He could have just sent me packing with those guards hunting me down," she pleads, and I see the tears shimmering on her lashes. "I... I don't know what I would do if something happened to him."

When she blinks, the tears that had been hanging onto her lashes fall. They trickle down her cheeks, but she swipes at them. The conviction in her expression tells me there's more to her connection with Donahue. Perhaps she's related to the man. I know he has never been married, which confirms he's probably never fathered a child. His brother on the other hand, isn't a priest. Perhaps this wee girl is his niece.

Sighing, I turn to the bike and grab my helmet. "Put this on," I tell Miren before swinging my leg over the bike and offering her my hand.

Once her body is nestled against mine, I start the engine. As much as I didn't want her on the back of my motorbike, I can't deny her wanting to see the priest.

He's always been sound to me, and if my deductions of their relationship are true, she'll want to see him.

There's no other explanation. She must be his niece. He would never have asked me to help her if he didn't care for her. There isn't any other conclusion I can come up with. If she were a stranger to him, he would've found a shelter in the city for her.

It feels as if this is the longest ride I've ever endured. I didn't expect her to wrap her arms around me. But why wouldn't she? She's on a fast-moving motorbike. I can feel the warmth of her, and the softness of her moulds to me, which has my hackles rising. It doesn't make sense that this stranger would ignite a fire inside me. I chalk it up to my self-imposed drought.

I got tired of the club whores who wanted a ring on their finger. I don't want an old lady, but they didn't get the hint. It brought me to a conclusion, every woman who slipped into my bed, no matter how much I told them it wouldn't lead to somethin' long term, wanted more.

I'm thankful when we pull up to Donahue's house. Even though it's in darkness, I notice the gates are wide open. He never leaves them unlocked. Usually, they're shut tight when he goes to bed. I recall one late night, my sloshed arse stumbled up to his house, and I had to bang on the gates to wake him up. He allowed me to sleep on his sofa, sobering me up with coffee.

I kill the engine and help Miren to her feet before I follow suit. Her soft footfalls behind me are the only sounds besides mine against the concrete tiles. I'm pretty sure she's holding her breath. I pull out my gun and unlock the safety before knocking on the door. But the moment my knuckles hit the wood, the door slides open.

My gut twists with anxiety. I know I'm about to find a dead body. There's no doubt in my mind. I know because I've come across scenes like this too many times to count.

"Stay behind me," I whisper as I step over the threshold. The entrance hall is empty, and I turn left into the lounge where I see him before Miren does. Immediately, I spin on my heel and stop her. "Stay right here. Do not come in this room."

Her eyes are wide as she stares up at me. "What's wrong?" Even though I can hear the break in her voice, knowing she has realised what we found, I shake my head.

Leaving her at the entrance, I move deeper into the room and crouch down. The body of Father Donahue is unmoving. And when I reach for his pulse point, I feel nothing. Someone killed him, and I have a feeling I know who it is.

A gasp of surprise behind me has me shooting to my feet. I turn to find Miren, hand on mouth, tears streaming down her face as she looks at the old man.

"Is... Is... Is he dead?"

I nod. There's no reason to hide it anymore. "Unfortunately."

Slowly, Miren falls to her knees, and a sob of agony falls from her perfectly plump lips. I tell myself I didn't notice them, I didn't truly examine every inch of her that I could, but it would be a lie. I did, and I don't know why.

"You need to be honest with me," I tell her, causing her to look up through wet lashes.

Her lower lip wobbles. "What do you mean?"

"Is Donahue yer uncle?"

For a long, silent minute, I'm pretty sure she's about to nod, but then she says, "No. He's an honest man who didn't deserve this."

The anger in her voice has me watching her reaction. If she's not his daughter, then there's something she's still hidin'. Perhaps I should keep her around. More time will allow me to learn who she really is.

First things first, I need to call Sergeant O'Malley. And then I'm going to take Miren home, let her work for us, and have Tye dig into her past. Those secrets need to be uncovered, and when they are, I'll make her pay for her lies.

CHAPTER NINE

Miren

I follow Callia around the club. It's not too busy yet, but the few club members that are here have girls on their laps with drinks in their hands. Thankfully, I'm able to observe before I start a shift.

"This is the main bar," she tells me as we reach the centre of the room.

It's got a wall filled with bottles of spirits, along with glasses, and shelving that's illuminated in a soft purple. The counter is dark wood, a veneer that shimmers under the low lights. It's not what I expected to find.

When someone says strip club, the immediate image that comes to mind is a dingy dive. But this is elegant.

Opposite the bar are round tables, with soft cushioned seating, and a large stage that looks like it's been created for a band. There's a pole smack dab in the centre, and it's the only evidence of what this place is. The waitresses are all dressed in black shorts and figure-hugging tees. However, they aren't showing off anything more than you'd see if they walked by you on the pavement.

"This is..." I look over at Callia who's currently assessing me. I'm not sure what to say.

This place is really nice. Even the clientele who are seated at the tables overlooking the stage are respectful. They may be shouting out *whoops* and *get on, ye lassie* but they're not grabbing at the girls.

"Not what you expected from a bunch of bikers?" Callia laughs when I nod slowly. "Told ya, yer man, Monster, is sound. Most of the eejits who walk in here are thrown out on their arses."

"I just didn't think it would be so..." I'm not sure what to say.

"Classy?"

"Yes," I mumble, and Callia laughs again before taking my hand and leading me over to the bar.

"You're welcome to sit back here and enjoy the night. Drinks are on the club, but don't get too drunk. Monster doesn't approve."

When I look at her, I notice a glint in her eye, but it's gone before I can ask what she means. She offers me a wave, and I know her shift starts soon, so I order a Coke and settle in. I observe the two girls who are currently on the stage. They finish up their routine just as another performer steps onto the platform. I can't deny she's beautiful.

Once I'm settled at the corner of the bar, I watch as the club gets busier. But my focus isn't on what's happening in the room, it's on the three men who enter shortly after another group of dancers start their routine on stage. Monster Rebel, and Sully saunter in. They're in charge, there's no question about it. Monster takes a front row seat, and even though I'm nothing to him and he's nothing to me, I can't help the shiver of resentment that courses through me.

Jealousy rears its ugly head when one of the girls offers him a smile. I don't recognise her from the club, but it's clear she's got her eye on the man in charge. She drops to her knees, toying with him as she wiggles around on the smooth, shiny stage. When she rolls over onto her back, she spreads her legs wide, and offers

Monster a clear view of the apex between her thighs.

The rest of the group cheer and whistle, but he doesn't react. At least, from my viewpoint I can't tell if he does, but he seems to sit so still I wonder briefly if he's asleep. But then Rebel throws a note onto the stage in her direction, and that's when Monster pushes his chair back and rises to full height.

The girl smirks when he leans in, his mouth right at her ear. I'm not sure what he tells her, but from the way her grin falters, it doesn't seem good. Monster turns and walks away, leaving the poor girl staring after him. The lads don't follow him, and I can't deny I'm intrigued.

When he steps out of the club and the door shuts behind him, I can't stop my feet from following. I shouldn't be doing this. He could find out who I am and have me killed, but my need to be near him is far too strong. I exit the noisy club and find Monster leaning against the brick wall, smoke billowing from his lips, and he turns his attention on me.

His gaze is heavy, dark, his scowl obvious. "You're meant to be inside," he tells me as he takes another long drag on his smoke.

"I wanted to see if you're okay," I say, suddenly unsure of why I want to be anywhere near this man.

He's grouchy. He's rude. And I know he doesn't like me.

He side-eyes me, his dark brow arching as he regards me. "You worried about me, wee fox?" His question startles me because he's never been other than gruff towards me. But the nickname he's given me makes my cheeks heat. All I can do is hope he doesn't notice I'm blushing.

"I just don't like seeing people upset."

"What makes you think I'm upset?" This time, he turns to face me fully. "You talkin' about the dancer in there?" I nod. "Aye, she wanted to ride my dick tonight. Are you offerin' as well?"

I step back in shock at his blatant question. My mouth drops open, but I force it shut because I have no response to throw back at him.

Monster takes a step towards me and leans in close. The spicy scent of his cologne feels as if it's draped over me, causing me to shiver at his nearness. "Unless that pretty little cunt you're hidin' is still pure and tight."

"You're filthy," I bite out as anger takes hold.

"Aye," Monster acknowledges. "Is that somethin' you like? Did Bragan's men get ye used to the fact ye're nothin' more than a toy to them?" His voice is so low it's practically a growl.

The idea of any of my father's soldiers being near me sends revulsion racing through my veins. From my short time in that hell hole and coming face-to-face with most of Patrick's men, I can't bear the thought of any of them desiring me.

I want so much to tell him who I am. Right now, I'm angry enough to come clean. He'll probably kill me, but I don't like him thinking I'm just some girl who's been passed around men who worked for my father.

"Is that how you see all women?" I throw back, hoping to knock him off-kilter.

When Monster looks at me, I see it in his eyes, a flicker of something, regret perhaps, but I can't be sure because it's gone the next second.

"Go inside," he tells me.

Folding my arms across my chest, I meet his rigid stare. I'm about to respond when gunshots ring through the night, one slicing against my arm, sending me to the ground with Monster covering me from the attack.

The club doors swing open, and there's more shots fired. This time I realise Rebel, Sully, and Racer have appeared, their focus on the fleeing motorbikes that rumble by. Once silence hangs heavily, I look up into the face of the man who I know hates me. Those dark eyes sear through me, and it's as if he's looking directly into my soul.

His gaze drops to my arm where pain radiates like a beacon, and I want to scream, but the sound is stuck in my throat. Monster moves off me swiftly before looking at the men who are now watching us.

"Get her inside." His order is gruff, and soon I'm on my feet with Rebel and Sully leading me into the club.

We make our way to the back rooms where I'm perched on a chair. Sully is examining my arm, but my eyes are on Monster as he shrugs his cut off, then pulls the T-shirt he'd been wearing up and over his head.

Every dip and peak of his muscles tense and release with the movement. I'm more than distracted by him when Sully suddenly presses on the wound, which is bleeding, and I cry out in agony. When I do manage to tear my eyes away from Monster, I find Sully standing beside me with a pair of tweezers. Pinched between the metal tongs is a small piece of metal.

"Bullet shattered. This was stuck in yer arm." The corner of his mouth tilts upward. "Brave girl." He turns and walks out as if he's just told me the weather is lovely today. They're so used to guns and violence it's no surprise we've just been shot at. But I have a feeling the target was me, not Monster.

Monster and Rebel turn their attention on me, but

it's Monster who speaks, "You need to come clean."

My mouth falls open in shock. "What?" I squeak, and I wonder what the hell they want me to tell them.

"Monster!" A woman shouts his name, and I pray he'll leave me be.

Sully returns with bandages and a first aid kit. The man looks at me, then Monster, and I can tell he's noticed the air in the room is charged with something dangerous. I have no doubt that the President of the MC will lose his mind when he learns the truth.

"Later," Monster tells me before walking out, leaving me with Sully.

There will be questions about why someone would be targeting me. All I wanted was to move on from my past life. Father Donahue is dead, and I have nobody else to lean on. Being with the club will provide safety, up until the day they find out who I really am.

"Hey," Sully says, capturing my attention. "Don't let him get to you. Monster may come across as a bastard, but he's a goodun," he tells me. "He won't kick you out on the streets if he knows you're in danger."

I stare at him for a long while. I'm unsure of what to say. I wish it could be different, that I didn't have to lie to them. But it's the only way I know I'll survive this. Getting out of here isn't going to work, not until I know for sure my father is dead. By then, Mum should have returned—she has to come back. Then I can head back to London and try to start a new life.

"I just don't want to be a bother," I tell Sully. "I'm only going to bring trouble down on the club, and that's the last thing I would ever want."

"Once you're in," Sully says then, "you can't leave."

"What if I don't belong?" I ask.

It doesn't go unnoticed how broken I sound, how scared I am. I don't want to talk any more. If I do, I may give away the fact I'm holding a secret, a dark and dirty one.

"Nobody belongs in the club," Sully informs me gently. "We're all just broken pieces fitting together. We make up a family, not by blood, but by loyalty. The code of the Royal Bastards runs deep."

"I just don't think I'm part of that family, that connection you guys have," I say, shaking my head as my words falter for a moment. "I'm not a part of it." I lower my head, focusing on the floor instead of the intense stare Sully is currently giving me.

His tender fingertips touch my chin, lifting my gaze to meet his. "You may think you're not part of the family or the club, but you are. You were the moment Monster allowed you into the house. When he agreed to let you work at the bar. Don't let his gruffness get to you," he tells me with a small smile curling his lips. "He's like that with everyone."

"I suppose so," I finally whisper. But I don't tell him the real reason I feel so nervous, so scared of the man who runs the club. I can't. "We better get back in there," I say, pushing to my feet.

Wincing at the pain radiating through my arm, Sully places his hand on my lower back and leads me out into the main area of the club.

We find the rest of the brothers surrounding Monster, who looks like he's raging. I don't at all want to be a part of it, but Sully doesn't let me go. Instead, he leads me right into the foray, and I'm suddenly the centre of attention.

Monster is the one who speaks first. "Who was that?" He gestures with his chin towards the door. "Who was tryin' to kill ye?"

There's no doubt in my mind it's my father's men, but I can't tell Monster the truth. Patrick's men know who I am, and they know he wanted me dead once he got the information out of me. Even though I couldn't give him much, I don't think they'll let me live.

I shrug. "I don't know."

"Don't lie to me," Monster growls as he takes a few

steps towards me.

The rest of the men watch intently. The music hasn't stopped, the show is still going on, and the clientele are focused on the women rather than the altercation happening right behind them.

"I'm not lying," I bite out. Tipping my chin upward, I square my shoulders and then lock my gaze on Monster's. "It could be Bragan's men, but they wouldn't want to hurt me. I was nothing to them."

"If you worked for the bastard, then they'll be gunnin' for you. What did you really do in that house?" This time, I have to look away from the intensity of Monster's glare. "Miren." He says my name slowly, testing it on his tongue, and I want to run.

I want to turn around and run away, but I can't because he'll find me. There's no place this man wouldn't look if I were to try to disappear. But I can't. Because the moment I attempt a getaway, my father's men will find me. I want so much to be free; I even thought I had my freedom, but I've only imprisoned myself in another home where I'm nothing more than a distraction.

I finally turn my attention on Monster. "I don't know why they would want me dead. I was in that house for a long time, but I didn't see anything. It's not like I was a witness to a crime."

"Get her back to the clubhouse," he orders, but he doesn't look away from me. His attention is locked on me as if he can carve out the answers he needs. Sully steps forward, and he walks with me.

We leave the club, and the night air has a chill in it. It's almost Christmas, and I'm alone with no family to speak of. I don't know how to get to my mother, not when I'm being watched so closely. And after the attack, I'm probably going to have a twenty-four-hour guard following me around.

"He'll come around," Sully tells me.

He brings me to the room I was offered on my first day, and he waits on the threshold of the bedroom. Inside, it's warm. With the heating on, the cosy atmosphere is so different to what it's like in the club.

I turn to Sully. "Thank you."

"Ach, there's no need to be thanking me," he says with a smile. "You get some rest. I'll be out here if you need anything."

"You don't have to—"

The look he gives me tells me that he'll be in worse shite if he leaves me here alone. "Just get some sleep."

And with that, he pulls the door closed, and I'm left alone. My arm still throbs from the pain, and my head starts hurting with a dull ache that I know won't go away with painkillers. It's guilt. It weighs on me.

The people here have been so welcoming, but I wonder what they'll do if they ever found out who I really am. As exhaustion takes a hold of me, I strip down to my underwear and slide under the covers. I'm too tired to do anything other than allow sleep to steal me.

I just have to get by until I can leave.

And it's with that thought my lashes flutter closed.

CHAPTER TEN

Monster

I watch her in the garden. She walks amongst the hedges Da had always kept in good condition. Her fingertips trail along the leaves, makin' them dance. When I first saw her, I was mesmerised by her beauty. I wanted to learn who this wee beauty was. My chest tightened when I thought about her in trouble, in danger. The need to protect took over and held me in a feckin' tight fits. But I pushed them away—those feelin's. I didn't need to be distracted when I had my focus.

I should have sent her packin'. But feckin' Donahue looked at me and asked straight to my feckin' face. Granted, I would have agreed because he's been good to me. For years I'd been broken. There was heartache that ran deep into my soul. And he knew it. He watched it happen as he laid Da to rest. And then, not too long after, he had to watch over Ma's funeral. He spoke of her with fondness, which I can never forget. Everyone who met my mother loved her.

Which brings my attention back to Miren. She's stopped to talk to a couple of the kids the old ladies brought to spend the day here while they work. She drops to a crouch, whispering in their ears secrets I'm not privy to. They giggle and nod at whatever she's told them, and I find myself jealous of their interaction.

I've pushed her away. I've made sure she knows she's not welcome here. But each time she's close by, in the same room, I can't help but look. Stare at her. There is a delicate beauty to her, but there's also a secret. Somethin' she's hidin'.

"You stalking the new girl?" Rebel says as he walks up behind me.

The bastard is far too pretty to be a biker. And I've told him that. Time and again. We've known each other for years, since I knocked him out in a pub one night. Arsehole was hittin' on a girl I wanted, so we did the manly thing and fought over her. I won of course. And that's when I knew we'd be friends forever.

It wasn't about the girl in the end. We became fast friends. All the men here, all my brothers are men I would die for. Rebel being my VP. Racer who's the youngest Road Captain the club has had. Banks, who handles our money, and Hadrian, also known as Rev, our Chaplain. Our Enforcer, Brute, is a dangerous motherfecker, and Sully who comes and goes because he's always out doing clean-up. Tye is the newest member, but he's patched, and I'm proud to have him in the family. He's our Tech, and he's feckin' good at what he does. Those are my men, and I would be lost without them.

"She's hidin'," I tell Rebel. "I don't like when I see secrets in someone's eyes."

"Aye? You've been staring into her eyes, have ye?" He nudges me with his shoulder, and I'm tempted to knock him the feck out again. Wouldn't be the first time, and I doubt it will be the last. I glare at him, my mouth tight with frustration. "Feck off," he throws out. "I know what you're like. I can tell when someone's got to ye."

"She's not got to me in any way, Rebel," I tell him.

"When there's a stranger in our home, I must be vigilant. I let down my guard, and shite hits the fan." There was only one person, a long time ago, I allowed in. And it ended badly. Not even a month into our connection, I would never call it a relationship, I found her with someone else. Not just anyone, but the president of a rival club.

"Not everyone is out to hurt you," Rebel informs me, his tone soft, gentle, as if he's talking to a child who's angry, throwing a tantrum. I look over at him and arch a brow. "I'm serious. I'm not saying you should trust her right off the mark, but ye can't live yer life alone."

"Aye, I can. You're just telling me this because she's a pretty wee thing. A fox, cunning, wily."

"There you go." Rebel shakes his head as he turns to leave. "Now why don't ye go catch a fox and tame it."

I listen to his boots walk off down the hallway, and I decide to follow the wee fox. Her dark hair has one lock of deep red that's only visible when the sun is shining on it.

When I reach the garden, I stop beside her. "Lovely day." Inwardly, I cringe at the awkward shite people talk about.

"It's nice. I didn't expect a garden like this so close to a large city. London is so different," she tells me.

"I'm guessing the centre of the city isn't far from here?" Those eyes, those feckin' eyes look right into me as if she's trying to find a path to my soul. I wonder what she'd do if she found it.

"Aye, it's about fifteen minutes up the road," I tell her.

I haven't been out there in a while. Maybe she wants to go shopping with the girls. I should get Racer to take Callia and Miren into town. They can buy whatever they need. One of the men will have to accompany them. I don't need Miren runnin' off.

"I'd like to go sometime. Maybe you could take me?" she offers with hope shining in those blue-grey eyes. They change colour as the sun is hidden by the clouds that have blown over. I can't spend more time with her. I'm already too feckin' fascinated by the girl.

"I'll get one of the brothers to take ye and Callia," I tell her.

Turning, I go to walk away from her, needing to put space between us. But her hand lands on my arm.

"I understand you don't like me," she says then, and I want nothing more than to argue that fact. It's the complete opposite, but she can't know how I feel. My need to be close to her, to protect her has taken over, and I don't know what the feck to do about it.

"What makes ye think I don't like ye?"

"I can tell. I've always been good at reading how people react to me, to situations. It's not difficult to see you don't want me here."

She stares at me. I wonder if she's willing me silently to disagree. I can't. As much as I think she's breathtakingly beautiful, I can't give her what she needs. If she is innocent, if she is just a victim in Bragan's games, then the truth will come out. But I can't trust her.

"My family are my life," I inform her. "Havin' ye here doesn't change that. I've helped many a youngen to find their way. It's nothing new. But I'm careful as to who I let in, who I allow to see the inner workin's of my world."

"I understand. I'm not a threat," she tells me.

Her lips curve, a slight pout to the lower one makes her seem younger than her twenty-two years. I don't care how beautiful she is though, she's not to be trusted. No matter how much I find myself drawn to her.

"Aye, that's what all the criminals tell me." I look away, focusing on the garden instead.

"I grew up alone with only my mother. Anyone who she brought home I saw as a threat as well. So, I understand. The moment I can, I'll leave." Her words are firm, confident. I don't argue with her. It will be for the best. At least she knows she has to go. Saves me from doin' it the hard way.

"Good." I turn once more and look at her one final time before headin' indoors. I can feel her eyes on me. They follow me everywhere I go. Two feckin' magnets that can't get enough of the attraction.

It's not good.

Not one feckin' bit.

The music fills the club. It's packed; heavin' with clients who are throwin' money around like they're swimmin' in it. I don't mind them pissin' their hard-earned cash in my club, though.

Miren strolls by me, her confidence in waitressing has grown, and watching her has become my new favourite thing to do. I swallow back a mouthful of my pint, the Guinness dark and strong, just how I like it. Sully saunters in, his eyes tracking each of the girls, but he doesn't focus on them for too long. I wonder what his story is. I know he's ex-army, been on the front line, but other than that, he hasn't talked much about any woman in his life.

He prefers his own space. He is one of two of the

brothers who don't live at the clubhouse, Tye bein' the other. Sully chooses to live in the city because he wants the hustle of Belfast. I can't deny, it's a drawin' card. At nearly thirty-five, he's had to ward off a fair few beauties. Those who want an older man in their beds.

"What's goin' on?" He settles in beside me and signals for a Jameson with a splash of cloudy lemonade. His signature drink.

I can't stand the shite. If I'm havin' a whiskey, it's neat. No feckin' ice, and none of that sugary drink to spoil the flavour.

"Not much. Money is comin' in. Drinks are flowin'," I tell him. "And the shipment will be comin' in soon, which means we'll see a payday."

"That's needed," Sully agrees. "Haven't had many clean-ups lately," he tells me. "I met with some 1%ers a few weeks ago. They're looking to move into Antrim."

"Oh, aye?"

"They seem sound enough. Tye didn't find any shite on them, so I'm guessin' they keep their noses clean. As much as they can." He gulps back his drink before ordering another. "Maybe we can have them here for a few days. It's always good to have connections we can use."

"Aye, I agree. I don't mind either way." I turn my

attention back on the stage where Heather is stepping up to do her dance. But my gaze strays over to where Miren is serving a table of blokes. They're drunk, which has me on edge. If any of the customers touch my girls, they lose a feckin' hand. It's in the rules. And these wee bastards look like they enjoy breaking rules.

Miren sets their drinks down, and one of them goes to grab her arm. I don't realise I'm movin' until Sully's grip on my collar drags me back down onto the bar stool.

"What the feck ye playin' at?" I growl at him.

"If you keep runnin' after the wee lass, everyone will get the wrong impression," he tells me with a grin on his face.

Cheeky fecker. He's right, though. I'm losin' my head over a girl I don't know. One I can't feckin' trust.

"Aye, you're right, but I can't allow feckers like that to take over our club," I tell him, and I note how he looks over at them.

Slowly, Sully releases me and smirks before he finishes his drink in one big swallow and pushes away from the bar. He saunters over to the table where Miren is still tuggin' away from the arsehole. Sully grabs him by the scruff and lifts him from the chair. In the process, Miren is freed from his hold, and I watch as my cleaner drags the wee bastard outside.

Miren looks up at me as our Enforcer, Brute, heads for the circle of friends, causing them to scatter towards the door. Chuckling, I shake my head and make my way to the back of the club. I need to finish some work in the office before I head home. I'll leave the brothers here to keep an eye on things. I know the girls will be all right.

I turn the corner, and something soft and delicate slams right into me. Blue-grey eyes flick up, and they lock on my stare. She's so feckin' beautiful, and fer a moment, I'm speechless being this close to her. There's a small freckle on her nose, and my fingers itch to touch it. To feel her soft skin, to see if it's as fragile and delicate as it seems.

"I-I... I'm sorry," she mumbles, her pouty lips shimmering in the dim light of the hallway.

She's shorter than me, her head coming up to my chest, and I imagine pulling her into my arms. Just for a moment. The idea sends heat zipping through every inch of my body, and I have to bite back the groan of need that warms me.

"For?" I arch a brow at her, pinning her with a stare.

"I... Nothing," she tells me then, tipping her chin back, but those eyes, they hold mine with confidence.

Her fire is slowly flicking to life, and I want to see when the inferno blazes through her. As I stare down at her, I realise just how much I want to make her explode.

"You should be at the bar," I tell her. "I don't pay you to hide out in the back."

"I'm not hiding. I came back here to freshen up," she bites out, gesturing with her hand towards the toilets.

I've made sure the girls have dressing rooms and a shower room with toilets where they can go if they need to catch their breath, top up makeup, or change their clothes.

When Miren turns back to me, she looks up, and her lips purse. Frustration dances in her eyes like a flame as she narrows them at me. *Challenge me, wee fox.*

"I know I'm here because you wanted to show the goodness in your heart, but you don't have to treat me like a bother each time you come close to me." Her tone is filled with annoyance, but mingled in with that is hurt. Her expression is pained, and I wonder if I really affect her as much as she does me.

"You are a stranger," I tell her. Tamping down my desire, I focus on who she is, what she's doing here. "The moment I know fer a fact I can trust ye, then I'll treat ye like family. Until then." I pause as I reach for her chin and grip it between my thumb and forefinger. "You'll be treated any feckin' way I want to treat you. Am I clear?"

Miren pulls away, and I immediately miss her soft skin under my fingertips.

"Then I'll leave," she says as she swans by me, and I grip her arm, stopping her in her tracks.

"You will not go anywhere," I tell her. "Those feckers are out lookin' for you. If you're willing to lose yer life because you want to act like a feckin' child, then I'll let you go. I'll drive you out into the city centre myself. But I've a feelin' that's not who you are."

She looks at me for a long moment, then she whispers, "I don't want to die."

Five words that grip my heart in my chest. The ache is unreal. I've never connected with anyone. Granted, I chat to the brothers and the girls who work at the club, but a deeper, truer connection has always evaded me.

"Then do yer job, listen when I tell you to do somethin', and come to terms with the fact that this may be yer home fer a wee while."

I release her, turn on my heel, and make my way to the office. The moment I'm inside the room with the door shut behind me, I pinch the bridge of my nose. My hand is still hot, zingin' with heat where I touched her.

And I wonder what it would be like to have her naked, writhin' beneath me as she takes my cock. To hear her whispers and whimpers, her moans, and to hear her beg for more. But right now, I need to focus on work. Not the pretty wee fox who's burrowed her way into my head.

CHAPTER ELEVEN

Miren

There's a party at the clubhouse tonight with the bikers, along with some of the girls from the club and a few hangers-on. Callia pulled me aside earlier and told me about the girls who would attend the parties to entertain the guys. There are a few club members who are single, and they're the focus for these girls.

I didn't think anything of it. They wouldn't bother me much, but then as I was getting ready, I realised she probably told me because they would flirt with Rebel. Callia's crush on him is evident, at least to me it is.

The two of them—Rebel and Callia—seem oblivious to each other. Unless they're hiding from it. The thought brings Monster to mind, and as much as I try to fight the images of him, I can't. He's focused on me because I'm still a stranger to him. I understand that his trust isn't something he can give freely. He found me in his enemy's home. But deep down, I want him to like me.

Shaking my head, I glance in the mirror and expertly line my eyes with the dark Kohl pencil. The black makes my eyes pop; the blue prominent tonight.

As I straighten, I spin around, taking in my reflection. The sleek black dress Callia loaned me fits like a glove. Luckily, we're the same size, and I'm able to borrow outfits from her. I've managed to order a few things, but I didn't focus on party dresses. Which brings me to Callia's dress. It's short, shorter than I would usually wear, but I think it looks good.

With a smile, I head out after slipping on the heels she's loaned me. Downstairs, the music blares through the speakers, along with the voices that filter up to where I am. I'm about to make my way down the stairs, but my arm is gripped by a strong, firm hand.

I glance over my shoulder to find Monster glaring at me. "What the feck are you wearin'?" he asks through his teeth.

The man is seething. He's practically expelling steam from his ears. I bite back a laugh as I picture it in my mind.

"A dress," I respond to him, which I realise may not be the best idea since he's not in a good mood. But I'm so tired of him ordering me around when he has no claim over me. We're not together. If I want to dress in a sexy outfit, and perhaps find someone who wants me, then so be it. He can't stop me.

"You'll go back to yer room and put some jeans on," he orders, his fingers still gripping me harshly. "Do it. Now."

"You can't tell me what to wear. You don't do it with any of the other girls," I retort, tugging my arm from his hold. "Why are you like this?" I bite out in frustration.

The man before me has my hands fisting at my sides. He takes a step towards me, his eyes practically glowing with anger. With each movement he makes, I move back. Even as my heart thuds wildly in my chest, I'm not scared of him. I may want to run, but it's because he makes me feel something. He makes me want to stay, to tell him just how much I want to be here, and I can't do that. I can't stay.

"I told ye once before," he speaks, his voice low,

commanding. There's no amusement in his tone, and I know I fucked up. "You're in my home, and that means, I'm meant to take care of ye."

His thick Irish brogue has me squirming. I didn't expect to ever want someone so much, but when Monster leans in, I want nothing more than for him to kiss me. I move away from the stairs, and my back hits the wall.

We've been tiptoeing around each other since I arrived. But when I move, so does he. If he's not close, I seek him out in the crowd. The man who tried to touch me a few nights ago was beaten to within an inch of his life. I have come to realise these men would do anything to keep the women safe. As much as it fills me with warmth, Monster frustrates me.

"I didn't think he would—"

His hand slams into the wall behind me, causing me to flinch. "Didn't think he'd want to feck ye? Or didn't think he'd want to run his hands all over ye?" The anger in his tone is tinged with something else—jealousy.

"Why do you care?" I throw out before I have time to think. Rage blazes in his eyes then, and I realise I've just angered the man they call Monster. "I'm sorry."

He reaches for my chin, pinching it between his thumb and forefinger. "If you think for one second you can talk to me like that and get away with it, ye're sorely mistaken, wee fox."

The nickname he's given me makes my cheeks heat. When he first called me that a few days ago, I couldn't respond. I wasn't embarrassed, but I didn't want to admit to myself how much I liked that he'd given me something that was unique to the two of us.

"Why?" I bite out. "You going to spank me?"

My retort has him chuckling. "Oh, darlin', I'll gladly put you over my knee," he tells me, and I know he's not joking. "Now," he says. "You be a good girl and get back to work. I have shite to do, and I can't do it knowing you're runnin' around with yer arse hangin' out while feckin' arseholes paw at ye."

He pushes away from me, the heat of his body gone, making me shiver. When he's far from me, I miss him. And when he's close to me, it feels as if I'm burning up. It's stupid. I realise I can't *want* a man like him. I've come from one violent person, and I cannot be with another.

He leaves. My chest is heaving from being so close to him. The scent of his cologne still hangs in the air, invading my senses. Ignoring his anger, and his order for me to change, I make my way down to the party. Deep down, I'm sure it's going to end with him in a rage, but if he hasn't laid a claim to me, he has no say.

When I reach the foyer, I turn left and find Callia watching me with an arched brow. She stops next to me and giggles lightly. She's probably heard what went down.

"I think someone has a crush," Callia says when she sidles up to me.

Even though we're in lockdown, the club bar is busy. With all the brothers here, even a couple of what they call nomads, it's packed, noisy, and the women who hang around seem to be enjoying the attention.

"What do you mean?" I look at Callia to find a glint in her stare as she side-eyes me.

"You and Monster," she says then, causing my face to flush. "I've never seen him lose his shite like that before. Granted, he's a grumpy bastard, but that was new to me. There have been fights in the bar before, in the club as well, but he's always allowed Rebel or Racer to take the lead."

"He's just being overprotective because I'm new."

"I was new once too." Callia looks away, and I follow her gaze. In the corner of the bar, I spot Rebel, the VP. "But Monster never came to my defence."

"And Rebel did?" This time, it's her turn to blush.

She nods. "He did." There's a sadness in her eyes,

though. Makes me think of unrequited love. The ache that coils deep inside your soul for that one person. But they never notice. The frustration of it must linger long after your feelings are gone.

I look back at Callia. "But you're not together." It's a remark that has her smile falling for a moment.

I shouldn't have said anything, but my observation was only that the men will defend us, but it doesn't mean they see us as anything more than projects. They enjoy the protective commands they offer, but it's only because they're trying to ensure our safety. I look around and find Rebel, then my gaze lands on the Monster. His face is pinched in anger. I'm pretty sure it's about me.

He made it clear he didn't like my outfit, and he made it very fucking clear he wasn't happy about me coming down here. But there aren't any men pawing over me as he put it. I think he's scared everyone off.

"Romance and the road don't always go hand in hand," Callia says with a sad tinge to her voice. "Rebel loves his bike more than he'll ever love a woman." She sighs softly, her gaze faraway.

I'm convinced she's a dreamer. There isn't anything that this girl can't do. I'm in awe of her. I think it's incredible she's able to still look at a man who doesn't want her and see someone who's worth the love.

Shaking my head, I look back at Monster and stifle a groan of annoyance. "Aren't all bikers like that, though?"

She looks over at me and smiles. "That they are, darling."

I want to ask more, to find out what happened between her and Rebel, but I don't. If she's ready to talk about it, I'll listen, but we're not close enough to get emotional. So, I leave it.

"I better collect the empty glasses and get them washed up. I don't have to tidy, but it will take my mind off things for a little while," I tell her.

Monster wanted me to get back to work, so I'll obey. For now. He may be angry, but I have a feeling it's not at me, it's because of me. Deep down, what Callia said has hit me. I busy myself tidying up, but I can feel his eyes on me. He tracks me, and I know it's also because he's trying to figure out what I'm hiding. Monster is observant, and each time someone asks about my past, I don't offer any specific details.

I don't know how much longer I have to stay here, how much longer I have before someone notices, or I slip up. But I need to keep my head down and focus on saving enough to get out of Belfast. It's going to be the safest option. If I can get back to London, I know my way around. It will be easy for me to disappear in the crowds that the Big Smoke has.

I wouldn't go back to the townhouse, and I certainly wouldn't want to contact any of my friends. It would put them in danger. But I have enough savings that I can withdraw without anyone knowing. It's a long shot, but it's still a plan. It's a solid one because it will be easy enough to do it. Now, all I need to do is bide my time and get out of here.

I've tried to glean information each time I'm around any of the brothers, but they're secretive. Of course, I understand they won't talk about work in front of a stranger. If I can figure out how much they know about Patrick and Mum, or if they've found out who I really am, I can run before I'm caught in the crossfire.

The thing about it is, if I leave now, the men who worked for my father will find me. They know who I am. When I was taken, I came across several different guards. It means they've seen my face, and if I were to escape, it wouldn't be difficult to find me. And Mum's associates have watched me grow up. I'm stuck between two dangerous options, and either way I go, I'm going to end up dead. However, in this instance,

I'd rather be with the devil I don't know than the one who gave me life.

CHAPTER TWELVE

Miren

I'm healing.

My arm is no longer aching each time I move it, and Callia and I have grown closer. I didn't think it would be possible, but I'm fitting in amongst the club members. Even Rebel and Racer are talking more to me now. There are other brothers who aren't as forthcoming, but I have a feeling it's part of their position at the club. Sully and I spend evenings talking about nothing at all.

Monster, on the other hand, greets me, but I can

still see the intrigue in his stares. A week has passed since the shooting, and yet, there have been no leads. At least, none that I've heard of.

"Hey," I greet Callia when I come down at six before making my way to the bar to grab a drink.

We're both working tonight from seven, which gives us an hour to relax. Before work, we tend to have a couple of drinks and talk about what she's been up to during the day. I didn't think I'd be bored, but I'm finding out that the more Lia talks about being at school and going into the city, the more I'm ready to start my life.

I want to make use of what I learned in my studies because I worked hard to achieve it. Deep down, the need to help people ensures I won't give that up. There's no way I can.

"Are you ready for tonight?" Lia asks as I settle into the booth opposite her with a chilled sparkling water. I don't enjoy consuming alcohol before work, so I stick to lemonade or water.

"Yeah," I tell her. "I heard it's going to be busy."

"A bachelor party," she informs me with a smile. "They always tip more than the regular punters. I think we'll easily walk away with a thousand between us."

"What?"

The shock in my voice makes her laugh. She nods slowly. "Aye, they're generous to the girls. Which is always good for us."

"Listen," I start, hoping my plan will go off without a hitch. "When you're next heading into the city, I'd like to come with you."

"No bother. My classes are running this coming week, then we're off for the Christmas break. I didn't expect it, but I'm looking forward to the time off."

Callia's been going to art school, and from what I've seen of her work, she's going to hit the art world big time. Her realistic sketches are incredible, so lifelike, if you were to pass them, you'd think they're photographs, not pencil sketches.

"Do you think Monster will let me go without a fucking chaperone?" I ask her with a laugh when I spot the man walking out of church. He's followed by the rest of the brothers, and I take each one in.

There's Blaze, who I've come to learn is the Sergeant-at-Arms, then there's Banks. He's the Treasurer and pays us for our work at the club each week. Both men are in their mid-thirties. Banks is greying already, with his hair being a sexy mix of salt and pepper. While Blaze has dark brown hair with fleck of auburn when he's in the sun. Tall, foreboding, and yet, they've been nice to me.

Rev and Brute are next to exit the room. Twins. Sexy as all hell, but scary as fuck. Hadrian, who is known as Rev, or the Reverend, is the Chaplain, and his brother, Hades, or better known as Brute, is the Enforcer. The two men are tatted from hands to neck. I'm not sure about the rest of them, but from what I can tell, their torsos are also inked up.

I'm learning who they are. But as much as the Royal Bastards have welcomed me into their home, there's still this uncertainty as to who I am.

"You can always ask," Lia says, dragging my attention back to her. When Sully walks out of the room, he makes a beeline for us. "Hey," Lia greets him with a grin.

"Girls," he says, looking at both of us as he pulls a chair over and spins it around so the back is leaning against the table. His legs on either side, he settles in and grabs the beer Callia was drinking.

"Hey!"

"You're working anyway," he tells her before swigging back the last few mouthfuls. "Good shite," he curses before setting the empty bottle down.

"Do you have to be such a savage?"

"Aye," he tells her. "It's why the ladies can't keep their

hands off me." With a chuckle and a wink, he pushes to his feet. "Be careful tonight," he warns. "The punters coming in may pay well, but they're handsy. So, watch yerselves out there."

"Aye, we will do," Callia says, and Sully nods, leaving us to get our arses over to O'Hagans.

As we walk out of the bar area, I can feel the heat of Monster's eyes on me. There's no doubt he's staring. I shouldn't look back, but I can't help myself, and when I do glance over my shoulder, I lock eyes with him. Darkness swirls in his watchful gaze.

"Come on," Lia says as she tugs my arm, pulling me behind her. As the door shuts, the moment is gone, broken. "You really like him," she says, catching my attention.

"What?" I flick my stare to hers, and she laughs.

"It's obvious." She shrugs, seemingly not bothered by the fact that I do have a crush on Monster. I don't want to admit it to anyone, not even myself, but when Callia looks at me, I don't say anything. "I knew it. Nothing wrong with it. He's hot. I mean, I am not interested in him at all, but I can see the appeal."

The van is waiting to take us to work, and as we slide in beside each other, the air is thick with her questions.

We sit in silence for a moment before I ask, "Do you

think he hates me?"

"I think he doesn't know what to do with ye."

It doesn't take us long to get to O'Hagans, and the parking lot is already mostly filled up when the van pulls up outside the entrance. There are two prospects at the door checking IDs.

Callia and I walk into the club, where only a small handful of customers are already seated in front of the stage. The music is playing, but I can hear her.

"I have a feeling the man is stunned by yer beauty. He's attracted to ye, which makes him put up barriers."

Shaking my head, I shrug. "I doubt that."

"Aye, he's been through shite. He doesn't spend more than one night with anyone, ever," she explains. "I think if you were to sit down and talk to him, get to know him, you'll see he isn't as bad as he makes himself out to be."

"He just always looks at me as if I'm an enemy."

"I wouldn't necessarily say enemy, but you have to remember everyone is a stranger until you befriend them." This time, I look into Callia's green eyes that shimmer with mischief. She's serious, though. I wonder if I could ever get through to him.

Shaking my head, I focus on getting ready. There are trays of glasses that need packing away, so instead of continuing our chat about Monster, I change the subject.

"What about Rebel?" I ask Callia.

Her soft giggle makes me smile. "He's... difficult."

I stop what I'm doing and look over at her. "Aren't all men difficult?"

"Aye, but I don't know if I can ever be with someone," she admits, and the sadness that flickers on her face makes my chest tighten.

I don't know what her story is, and I'm too afraid to ask. We haven't really had deep heart to hearts yet. Mainly because I don't want to get attached to her and then leave. I can't imagine what that could do to her.

Or me.

"You never know," I say softly.

We work in silence after that, which leaves me time to consider what I'm doing. There's a constant twisting in my gut when I think about them finding out who I am...when Monster finds out who I am. The need to want him to accept me is a constant reminder of the affect he has on me.

"What's going on in that head of yours?" Callia stops to look directly at me.

I sigh because I know she won't stop until I've told her something. And even though I can't tell her everything, perhaps I can offer some hint of how I'm feeling. The thing about it is, I don't want her to tell Monster anything about me; at least, anything more than he already knows.

"I was just wondering if I should try to contact some long-lost family," I finally say.

It's not a complete lie, but it's also nowhere near the truth. I don't know where Mum is, and there's no way for her to contact me since Patrick took all my personal belongings.

"So you do have family?"

I look at Lia. "Yeah, kind of," I say with a shrug, but I don't elaborate because I can't.

Callia smiles then. "That's why we make such a good family here, love," she says. "Because we're all a little bit lost. Family doesn't always have to mean blood or genetics. It can just be the loyalty from those around you."

Our conversation is interrupted by the other girls walking in. The dancers who will take to the stage offer us a wave, and I'm thankful for the intrusion. As much as I do believe they're a close-knit group, I can't tell Lia that I just don't feel as if I'm part of it.

Because I'm not.

I'm the enemy.

As the night wears on, I serve drinks to the group of men who are in for the bachelor party. There are at least twenty of them. Between Callia and me, they've kept us busy. Back and forth with shots and pints of Guinness that they seem to swallow back far too quickly.

"Hey, gorgeous," one of them calls out when I set the drinks down on the table.

I offer a quick smile, but I don't engage. One thing Callia taught me was to allow them to shout and catcall all they want, but never to engage. It only makes them more willing to take things further.

"My mate is talking to you," the other guy to my left says.

Once again, I offer a smile and straighten, hoping to escape, but suddenly, I'm pulled backwards. Hands on my hips tighten, and no matter how much I try to escape, I can't.

"I said, hey gorgeous," the guy says as he settles me on his lap. Fear slams into me when he leans in, and the alcohol on his breath makes my stomach turn. I want nothing more than to get away, but the more I fuss, the more he laughs. "I thought girls like you like this shit," he sneers into my face.

"Please let me go," I ask, hoping that my calm tone

will be enough. It isn't.

He trails his hand down to my thigh, and as I shut my eyes tight, I pray. I have never been religious. I don't go to church, haven't been in a long while. As he reaches between my legs, bile rises to my throat, but then, in the next second, the hand is gone and his groan of agony echoes through my thoughts.

I snap my gaze open and find Sully glaring down at the bastard while I'm being lifted over someone's shoulder. I can't tell for a moment who it is, but when he moves, the scent of his cologne invades my senses. Monster.

"Get that fecker out of here before I feckin' kill him," he orders and walks towards the back of the club with me over his shoulder.

"Put me down," I shout, hoping he'll hear me over the music. I'm taken to one of the private rooms and set on the sofa. "What the hell was that?"

"You were violated," Monster says. "I have very few rules when it comes to the club, to the dancers, and the staff. They are not to be touched, groped, or even feckin' looked at the wrong way."

He's fuming. I finally have a moment to look at him, and I've never seen anyone this angry in my life. Not even my own father.

"I could've handled myself."

"The fuck you could," he growls, stopping short and leaning in, his face inches from mine. His gaze drops to my mouth for a moment too long before he flicks those dark orbs to mine.

I push up from the sofa and realise it's a mistake because now our bodies are flush. Every hard dip and peak of Monster's torso is against mine. But I don't lower my gaze to take him in. I can't get distracted by the beauty of this man. He's bad for me.

"Don't try to save me. Don't act as if you care."

Anger flashes in his eyes. His hand reaches for my face, and he squeezes my cheeks together, making my lips pout. And I don't miss the flicker of desire that burns in his stare before he looks into my eyes once more.

"If ye live under my roof, you're my responsibility. I promised Donahue I'd keep ye safe, and I intend on keepin' my word."

I can't respond. He knows I can't because the corner of his mouth tilts when he watches me attempt to retort. For a long, silent moment, we stand glaring at each other. I'm not his. I do not want to be some possession kept locked up in a glass box. I'm stronger than that, and I will fight for my freedom, even if it means fighting Monster for it.

Monster releases me, then steps back, and I'm thankful at the reprieve of his commanding demeanour. But he's not far away. He's still so close I can practically feel his body vibrate with emotion.

"I'll leave."

"Like feck you will," he throws back. "You'll stay in the house until we find the bastards that did this."

No matter how I want to argue, I know now I'll never be able to go into the city with Callia. My plan is thwarted. Each time I think I'm taking a step forward, I end up taking two back.

I wish I had my phone. Even if I did have my mobile, I couldn't use it because I don't know where my mum is. I could bring more trouble to the club; I can't do that to the Royal Bastards. They took me in, gave me a home when they didn't need to accept a stranger into their house. I won't put them in danger.

"Monster—"

"I'm not arguing with you," he tells me. "C'mere to me," he orders quickly. "I'll get you back home."

When I don't move, he glances at me from over his shoulder. Those dark brown eyes that remind me of warm cocoa pierce me. I want so much to tell him the truth. I know Monster hated my father, I'm not sure why, but I can only assume they were in a war of sorts.

"It's not my home." My whisper has him turning on his heel. He doesn't approach me, giving me the space I need.

"When I told Donahue you could stay with us, I meant it. You may not feel at home yet," he tells me slowly. "But it will come."

"I know you hate me, and I—"

"There was only one person in this world I ever hated," Monster interrupts. "And it's not you." Even though he doesn't say it, I know he means my father. "Are you coming?"

I nod because I have no choice. I have nowhere else to go. All the money I had saved while living with Mum is sitting in an account I cannot access. If I were to go to a bank, I could be tracked. My father's soldiers would find me. I recall the shots fired at me and Monster, and a cold shiver races down my spine. *They already have.* I shake the thought from my mind.

As we exit the club, I can feel every pair of eyes on us. They're all convinced Monster has feelings for me or is attracted to me. And him escorting me home, I'm sure, will only solidify their suspicions.

I don't know what's going to happen, but for now, I appease the man and settle on the back of his bike.

Being so close to him makes me feel something I don't want to, but I can't stop myself from the emotions.

As the rumble of the engine comes to life and we race out of the lot, I hold onto Monster even tighter. It's not far to get home, and deep down, sadness washes over me that it wasn't a long, winding journey. I like him, I want him, and there's no longer denying it.

I don't think it's a good idea to allow my feelings to take over, but as we come to a stop at the clubhouse, I know that if he were to kiss me right now, I wouldn't stop him.

CHAPTER THIRTEEN

Monster

We stop outside her bedroom, and it takes all my restraint not to lean in and kiss her. She watches me as if she can read my mind. Perhaps she can. The corner of her mouth tilts upwards, just slightly, and the small smile that curls her lips makes me want to steal it with my own.

As much as I don't trust her, I can't deny she's breathtaking. Incredibly beautiful. She's become a distraction because when she's in the room, I can't *not* look at her. And when she's not around, I want nothing more than for her to walk in. I want to feast on her with my gaze, even though I know I can't have her.

"Thank you," Miren says softly with her gaze averted.

She looks to the floor as I lean against the doorframe. I want her eyes on me. I want to look deep into them to find all the secrets she's hidin'. But when she does land them on me, all I can think of is wantin' to see them glisten as I make her come.

"Get some rest," I tell her, my voice raspy when I speak. "Tomorrow is another day."

I push away from her room and step back into the hallway. I want to say more, but I don't because I'm feelin' things I shouldn't.

When I turn around, but her voice comes from the threshold to her room to stop me. "If you push people away, one day they'll leave, and you'll be alone."

Her warnin' stops me dead in my tracks. The soft light from inside the bedroom illuminates her figure casting a shadow on the carpet before me.

I don't know why my muscles tense at her words. Anger warms my blood, and my veins seem to throb in every inch of my body. I'm not angry at her, but the fact that she's right. I know she is. It's somethin' Ma used to tell me. To stop pushin' people away. But it's the only way to ensure I'm safe from the pain of losin' them.

I turn my head, lookin' at her from over my shoulder. "You don't know me," I tell her earnestly.

She shakes her head. "I know, but I know when someone is hurting," she says. "Pain makes people do things they normally wouldn't. It makes you want to be alone, to never be hurt again. I understand that."

"You don't understand anythin'," I bite out as my anger slowly turns to fury.

Fisting my hands at my sides, I dig my nails into the palms, the bite of pain reminding me of why I live my life as I do. My brothers are the only people I care for, and even then, I know it's a mistake. I shouldn't allow myself to love, to feel.

"What I understand, what I see, is a man who's hurting," she says then, the confidence in her tone making her square her shoulders. "All I'm saying is that pushing others out of your life will only force you to feel more alone."

I turn to face her fully. Taking slow steps to her door, I stop on the threshold once more, but I don't move to touch her. I'm not sure I'll be able to restrain myself if I do.

"You think you know me, wee fox?" I ask her, tipping my head to the side to regard her.

She's a full head shorter than me, and she has to look up at me when I'm so close. The thought of her being fragile under me, begging me to show her mercy as I make her come, over and over again, flashes through my mind.

"I can read people." When she folds her arms across her chest, my gaze drops to the gentle slopes of her tits that peek at me from the low neckline of her tank top. My dick jumps at the sight, throbbing with the need to slide between them, to see her take every inch of me.

"You can't read me, darlin'," I tell her as I bring my stare back to hers.

She's confident in this moment. More so than I've seen her before. I'm impressed she's not cowerin' from my presence. Most women are either wanting to jump on my dick, or they're scared of me. But then again, my reputation precedes me.

"Why are you so scared?" she asks.

Without thinking, I stalk towards her, making her stumble back. We're in her bedroom, but I can't think about anything else right now. The only thing on my mind is pinning her against the wall. When her back hits the smooth surface, a whimper of shock falls from her plump, cherry blossom lips. I slam my hand against the hard wall behind her, and a squeak escapes her mouth.

"Are ye scared, wee fox?" I sneer as I lean in, and I'm immediately regretting this because the scent of her perfume invades my senses. My cock is thick against the confines of my jeans. "Because you feckin' should be." I tell her no word of a lie.

"What a-are you going t-to do to me?" she whispers, her voice stutterin' on the question.

Her eyes are wide as she watches me, as if she's taking in the image of me so close to her. I don't know what it means, because it's been so long since I've been close to a woman. I'm so close in fact I can practically taste her fear.

My self-imposed celibacy means I don't have to deal with the shite that comes with the club whores who want more than a one-night stand. The thing about Miren is, she's a far cry from that. She's so much feckin' more it hurts.

Ever since I first laid my eyes on her, the only thing that's been racing through my mind is the idea of fuckin' her. Of having her splayed under me, takin' my cock. And right now, feelin' her soft curves against me, it's a dangerous game.

"I'm not scared of anyone," she finally mumbles.

As much as I want to call bullshit, I can't. There's no

way this woman is afraid of anythin'.

"Why?" She's still hidin' somethin'. There's no doubt about it. I want to know what it is.

Deep down, I want her to confess all those sins to me. Miren knows more than she's told us. A nigglin' idea continues to plague me, one I don't want to think about. But each day I'm around her, I can't stop it from invading my thoughts.

"Because my mother taught me to never be afraid of monsters," she bites out. Her words send heat coursin' through me. And I want nothing more than to show her a real-life feckin' monster.

"Oh?"

"She taught me to be strong, to face my adversaries, and fight for what I want. There's no backing down, especially when you're a woman." She nods quickly.

Her lips purse, and I can't stop my mind from runnin' wild with images of my cock partin' them. I want her to take all of me. Swallowing every inch, she'll look up at me with those magic eyes, and she'll beg for more. I haven't ever been so attracted to a woman I both wanted to kill and wanted to fuck before. None of the whores who hang around the club have made me crazy like this stranger does.

And even though I want nothin' more than to see

her cry, it's her fire that has my blood heatin'.

"Good lady," I tell Miren. And it's true. There's nothing more I respect than a strong woman. Just like Ma was.

"She was," Miren says, and there's a tinge of sadness in her tone. Her gaze lowers to the floor.

Guilt rides through me like a storm. If I've spoken out of turn, I have to apologise, but first, I ask, "Was?"

Miren looks up at me again. The silver shimmering against the blue in her irises. "I don't know where she is."

I let out a breath I'd been holding and nod. "I'm sorry to hear that. If we can help in any way..."

I allow my words to trail off because I don't know why I'm offerin' this girl anythin'. She'll be gone soon. I don't want her here. She needs to know that. But the more I spend time around her, the more I can't stop myself from wanting to lean in and steal her lips.

"I'm worried. I wonder if she's okay," Miren tells me. "We have never gone this long without talking, so I'm just struggling with it. No contact may mean so many things."

I have nothing to say to that. Usually, I have answers for everything, especially when it comes to life and family. Ma always made sure I remembered everything she'd said to me. And I lived by many of her rules, all her anecdotes, but for Miren, I have nothin'.

"I'm sorry." The two words don't seem to be adequate, but I mumble them anyway. Then the corners of her lips tip upward, and she gifts me a smile that makes my heart thud against my ribs.

I don't understand why this girl has such an effect on me, but she does. And I know there's nothing I can do to stop it, not unless I force her to leave here. As much as I want that, I can't. She's helpless in a world filled with danger. Then again, I'm sure I'm the worst she'll come by.

"Thank you for everything," Miren says, dragging me back to the present and the fact that her feckin' cherry perfume fills my senses. "I don't know what I would do if they found me."

"Bragan's men will not come into the compound, so you stay here as long as you need," I inform her before I'm shocked speechless when she leans up on her tiptoes to kiss my cheek. Her lips send a zap right down my feckin' spine, and my cock throbs against my zipper. Coming into contact with her is more than erotic, sensual, or anythin' like that. It's a feckin' drug; heroin shot right into my veins. And I'm high as fuck.

She moves back, but I grab her arms and drag her

closer. "Didn't yer ma teach you not to go around kissin' strange men?" I ask her in a low tone that vibrates through my chest. From the tremble that runs through her slim frame, I can tell she feels it too.

No matter how much I fight this, I can't stop myself from leaning in and darting out my tongue. Gently, I trace it along her lips, tasting the sweet, alluring flavour of the stranger I've come to ache for.

"She did," Miren whispers. "But she didn't warn me against men I want to have kiss me." Her voice is a feather-light touch along my mouth, and the taste of her has my cock hard, ready to drive deep into her body.

"Ye should be careful, wee fox," I tell her. "Monsters eat girlies like you for dinner."

The warning has her eyes widening, but there's no fear flickering in the stormy stare she gifts me. Instead, there's lust, desire, and need. She emanates it like a goddamned perfume.

"Is that a promise?" Miren tilts her head to the side.

The corner of her mouth tips into a coy smile. One that I want to steal and swallow. Her body is flush against mine, and I know for a fact she can feel my erection.

"Ye don't want me to devour ye," I tell her. "Cause

when I'm done, there'll be nothing left."

Now she grins. "Perhaps that's what I need. To start afresh. To be someone else."

Her words send warning bells through me. If she's so adamant to change who she is, I need to find out the reason why. I step back and release her. The moment is gone. I can't do this because I can't trust her. Allowing myself to fall into a trap is unwise. Once I find out the truth about her, maybe I can let myself go. But right now, there's no lettin' down my guard. She's dangerous, more so than I am, because she's a feckin' siren.

"Go to bed," I tell her and turn away. I need time alone.

Leavin' her in her room, I make a beeline for my wing of the house. I have my own bedroom and bathroom with an entrance staircase that allows me to escape without being seen. In the sanctuary of my room, I lean against the door and shut my eyes. My head rests against the wood.

The taste of her is still on my tongue. If her mouth is so delicious, so intoxicating, I can't imagine what her cunt tastes like. I can't allow myself to even wonder. Considering the thought of havin' her for myself is dangerous.

I strip off and head into the attached bathroom and

turn on the shower. The only thing I can do now is calm myself down, that and my raging erection. My cock weeps for her, but instead of going back to the bedroom and fuckin' her, I step under the cool spray and grip my shaft.

Slowly, I stroke myself. I shut my eyes and think about her. I recall the way she kissed me. How her lips tasted. The gentle curves of her frame against mine. I'm lost in pleasure as my hand moves faster. Everything about the feckin' girl is what I want and need.

I tighten my grip, wondering how her cunt will feel as I fuck her. Will she pulse around my shaft? Will she milk my dick? The idea of coming inside her, of filling her with my release, sends heat racing down my spine, and I spill my seed against the tiles and watch it wash away with the water. Down the drain where it belongs. I can't be with her. She's forbidden fruit that I don't intend on taking a bite of any time soon. Or ever, I tack on at the end of my thought.

When I lift my eyes, I see a flash of long, dark hair, and then it's gone. I'm sure I'm hallucinating now. It's not her. It can't be. She wouldn't have watched me do that. But if she did, I wonder what she's feeling right now.

I turn off the taps and step out of the shower. With

a towel around my hips, I head to the bed and pick up my phone from the bedside table. I send a message to Tye, asking him to get all the information on Miren Doyle on my desk first thing in the morning. Anything and everything he can find. I don't care if it's one sentence or ten pages. I need it.

I do need to rest, though. I'm exhausted. I'll call church in the morning. We'll sit down and figure out just where we go from here. And then I'll bring Miren into my office, and she'll be forced to confess whatever it is she's hidin'.

I thought for a moment earlier she was goin' ta, but instead, she kissed me.

Once I'm in bed, I lie on my back and stare at the ceiling. But I can't sleep. My thoughts, instead, are on the girl down the hall. And I realise her kiss will forever be a mark on the monster.

CHAPTER FOURTEEN

Monster

"Jameson called with some info," I tell the brothers at the table. "It seems Bragan's wife has more responsibility than we initially thought. He had some contacts hack into the MI5 and Scotland Yard database, and her pseudonym Amanda Walsh has gone into hiding because she's not just his wife."

I look at each man. The news I found out this morning has not been sitting well with me. My gut is twisted in agony as I consider what this means. For years, I'd been going after the wrong man. Well, not entirely. I've been going after someone who was merely an instrument.

"What do you mean?" Rebel asks as he leans back in his chair to regard me.

I push to my feet and make my way to the printer where I left the documents that I printed off for them. I didn't want to tell anyone about this, but we can't stop the shite about to hit us. I set the pages on the table and push them over to Rebel.

"Take one and pass it on. We always thought Bragan was the head of the Irish mob."

Rebel looks up at me, shock clear on his face. "It wasn't him. It was her."

I nod. There's no denying it, because I can't. I made an assumption. It was wrong. I was wrong. The silence hangs heavily in the room. I don't feel guilty for going after Bragan, but even after digging into his organisation all these years, I never found out about Sinéad. She was nothing more than an ex-wife I figured escaped his clutches.

"She ordered the hit on yer ma?" Sully asks as he stares at me.

"Aye," I finally respond when I can look at them. "I fucked this up."

"You didn't," Racer throws back. "The Irish mob were

behind the killing. It doesn't matter who pulled the trigger, or who ordered the hit." His tone is confident, his words adamant.

"I was too focused on Bragan and not on the organisation," I tell them. "I wanted revenge."

"And we will get it. We will get her," Blaze, my Sergeant-at-Arms, says with confidence. "You can't blame yourself for the focus you had. If I were in yer shoes, I woulda been the same," he admits. "This," he murmurs, waving the page with the information in the air, "is enough for us to refocus."

"There's somethin' else," I tell them. "When I found Donahue's body, I called O'Malley, and he said there was no sign of Bragan leaving Ireland. Not even to head down to Dublin. Which means he's still close."

Racer asks, "We can go into the city and talk to some of the men?"

"We should also head north. Two of you take Antrim, while two of you ask around Belfast city. Someone must know something." I wasn't sure about it at first, but when I sat down to consider the reasonin', somethin' has been nigglin' at me. "Also, I have a feelin' Sinéad is comin' home."

"Do you really think she'll come home when she knows Patrick wants her dead?" Rebel looks at me, his brows furrowed in confusion. At first, I didn't think so, but I my gut tells me there's more to this than meets the eye. Walkin' out on soldiers who can protect her doesn't make sense. *Why run?*

Nodding, I sit back. "I think so," I tell him honestly. "I'm convinced she won't just leave her organisation in the hands of Patrick."

"And if Bragan is still alive," Rebel says, "we'll get him and his wife."

"You're talkin' about takin' down the whole feckin' Irish mob," I respond. My surprise must be clear on my face when he chuckles.

"Aye," he says. "What of it?"

The nonchalant shrug of his shoulders has us all staring at him. He's always been the one who asks questions after the fact. I've tried to steer him right, to teach him that a plan should be in place before executing any action. But Rebel has scars from his past that nobody knows about. It's not my place to tell them. So, instead of fighting with him, I've let him have his way. To an extent.

"What I don't want is any one of my brothers dead," I tell him, then proceed to focus on each and every man at the table. "If those feckers come near us, they won't think twice about pullin' a trigger."

"Then we pull ours first." Rebel is on his feet. His hands on the table with his eyes locked on mine. "Do ye think I'd walk away from this?"

"No, I don't think so. Feckin' hell, Rebel, ye got a death wish?" He doesn't move when I pin him with a glare. I don't like arguin' with my men, but he's pissin' me off. "Sit down." The order is clear, and for a moment, I'm certain he's goin' ta fight me on it. But then Rebel seats himself. "Now," I start, looking at my brothers are seated around the table which takes up most of the room. "We need to play this carefully. There's more to Bragan and Sinéad than we thought. If she's runnin' things from the States, and he's here carryin' out orders, we need a plan. One that's not goin' ta get us killed."

"Then we get a plan in place." Sully nods as he looks at the page of intel. "First thing I think we should be doing is stockin' up on guns. If these feckers think they can walk in here and take us down, they got anotha think coming."

"We can head down to the pier, talk to a few contacts, and see if they've seen any feckers hangin' around askin' questions," Rebel suggests, his tone less stressed than it was earlier. I don't want him getting hurt, and I'm thankful he's calmed the feck down.

"Take Sully and Racer with you," I tell him. "Tye, I need you to get flight plans, travel arrangements, anythin' you can on any of the mob moving around. Especially Sinéad. If we can find her, we'll be able to get things rollin'. I want to bring her in alive."

"Torture?" Blaze asks.

"Aye." I nod. "She needs to be questioned. I doubt she'll talk at first, so we'll need to keep her in the basement. The warehouse can be accessed by the mob if they want to get in. If we have her on-site, we can keep an eye on her."

"What about the girl?"

I realise now that I haven't told the brothers about what Miren and I found. Donahue is gone. I haven't even sat down to process the information. There's been too much to focus on all at once. We've been so concerned about finding Bragan's wife, that we didn't talk about Donahue being dead.

"There's something else," I say slowly. Most of the lads here grew up in Donahue's church. They attended mass, did their confirmations, and went to Sunday school where he would have his deacons teach us about the Bible. This was well before we stepped into the roles we have now.

"What is it?"

I look at Rebel. He can tell it's bad because I can't find the words. I didn't want to focus on the death before I could give them more answers. But since O'Malley called this morning and told me they've hit a dead end, I want us to look into it. I need Tye to dig into the priest's background and see what it is he was hidin'. It had to be something serious to have gotten him killed.

"I found Donahue's dead body a couple of nights ago," I explain. "I'd called him twice, and when he didn't answer, I went to his house. He'd been murdered."

"Was that the night you and Miren went off on yer bike?" Sully asks.

Nodding, I look at him. "Aye, she wanted to see the priest. I couldn't deny her since he was the one who asked us to take her in."

"What happens now? Will O'Malley investigate?"

"He called this morning to tell me they've hit a dead end. Tye—"

"I'm on it, Pres," he says with a salute.

"Anythin' else?" I look around the room, and none of the others raise their hand. It's been a tough few days, but we have to stay ahead of the shite before it hits us at home. I slam the gavel on the table and the screech of chairs echoes in the room. "Tye," I call to my

184

hacker. "Hang back."

Once we're alone, I motion for him to settle into Rebel's seat for the moment. We each have our own seats around the table, and no member can sit in another's without permission.

"I need you to do somethin' for me. The others don't have to know."

"Anything," he tells me.

"Miren. I need everythin' you can find on her. And I mean everythin'. I don't care if it's sensitive, personal, or private. She's hidin' somethin', and we need to know if she's a threat. If she's a mole, I want her dead." Even as I say the words, I wonder if I could bring myself to kill her. I've never hurt a woman before, never considered harming one, but with Sinéad being the mastermind behind Ma's death, I realise women are just as dangerous as men. At times, more so.

"I'll work on it now. If I find something..."

"Bring it to me, I don't care what time of the day it is," I tell Tye who nods and pushes to his feet.

"No problem, Pres."

When he leaves, I'm left alone in the room where we hold church every morning. Untangling all the shite with Patrick and his wife isn't going to be easy. My focus is torn between revenge and Miren.

I would much rather be out on the open road than stuck indoors. Being on the bike calms me. Even the strip club doesn't bring me joy anymore. Maybe I'm gettin' too old for this shite.

But I opened O'Hagans because I wanted the men to have a place of sanctuary where they can enjoy themselves. But also, to bring in money for the club. Our only other revenue stream is dealing in weapons, which means the two shipments coming in would be essential for us, one to stock up and another to sell on. And Bragan, or his wife, would know that. Sighing, I push to my feet and head into the bar area where I spot Miren. She's not working tonight. It's time she and I had a little chat.

"Miren," I call to her. Those eyes land on mine, and I notice the flicker of fear. "We need to talk." I turn around and head back into the room where I settle in my chair. She needs to give me answers. I'm not goin'ta allow her to keep feckin' secrets anymore. I'm done waitin' around.

The moment she steps into the room, her feckin' perfume follows along. When I got home the other night, I could smell it all over me. She'd been snuggled up against me on the bike on the drive to and from Donahue's place, and I couldn't get the fragrance off me.

"Sit."

"Is something wrong?" The concern on her face creases her brows. Her mouth tilts downwards at the corners, but it doesn't hide the beauty that shines from her.

"Tell me how you know Donahue, and don't claim it's because he's been yer priest. I want to know why you were at Bragan's house. And don't give me the same story the priest told me." I sit back and regard her. The flinch of her lashes, the way her hands curl in her lap is a clear indication that she's worried. I may have found a weak link in her story. It's Donahue. He may have told me she was kidnapped, but somethin' doesn't add up. The clothes she was wearin' were expensive, that much I figured out. I asked Callia, and she confirmed it.

"I told you—"

"Don't fuckin' lie to me!" The roar of my voice would have been heard in the bar next door if not for the soundproofing. Miren cowers, which confirms my suspicions.

"Pres!" Suddenly, the door flies open, and Tye stalls all movement on the threshold of the room. His gaze flickers between Miren and me. He's holdin' onto pages that, I'm guessin', contain the information I wanted.

"What is it?"

He looks concerned as he flicks his gaze between us. But I notice how he stares at Miren for a long moment, which sets me on edge. "I can come back."

"What is it, Tye?" I enunciate each word slowly, but I don't look at him, my focus is on the girl who's trembling in the chair diagonally opposite me.

I turn my attention back to him, and I focus on the fact that he still hasn't spoken up. I push to my feet and his stare turns to mine.

"I... Fuck..." He closes the distance and hands me the documents that, I'm assuming, he's just printed from the computer. I pick them up and drop my gaze to the information. The moment I pick out why Tye is so nervous, I drop the pages to the desk and settle back in my chair.

"Cheers, Tye."

"If you need—"

"I said, thank you, Tye," I reiterate my statement.

He nods and offers one last look at the girl sitting across from me before he turns and leaves, shutting the door behind him. Silence hangs heavily in the room. There's no doubt in my mind she would have picked up on the details because the pages aren't far from where she's seated.

"Monster," she whispers my road name. The one I was given when I took over the club. It's the one that everyone calls me. All my closest friends.

"Care to explain why you've been lying to me?" I say slowly. I haven't yet told her about my connection to her father. Or her mother for that matter. The realisation that's slowly dawning on me is that it was Miren's mother who ordered the hit on my family, on my mother.

"I don't know what you mean," she tells me, but I can see the lies flickering in her pretty, stormy eyes.

I need to tamp down my anger because I want nothing more than to pin her to the wall and force her to tell me everything.

"If you lie to me once more," I say, slowly, "I will bind you to the feckin' chair and torture you until you tell me what I want to know."

I push my chair out slowly, and the legs scrape along the wooden floor. Miren winces at the sound as it echoes in the room. I've been angry before, but that was all concentrated on my enemies. It seems, though, the wee lassie is one of those. She should be on the list of those I want to see dead.

"Please," she pleads with me. Her wide eyes piercing

mine as her lips tremble. "He was a stranger to me until a few weeks ago. I had never set foot in his house, and I never spoke to him before then." She looks directly at me as she says this, and I see no lie in her gaze. "I'm not lying to you, Monster. You must believe me."

I close the distance to where she's seated. I grip the arms of the chair and lean in until I'm inches from her. The warmth of her quick breath fans over my face. Fear dances like flames in her eyes. The storm is raging, the blue turned completely grey, and the way her lower lip trembles only seems to wake the monster I keep deep inside.

CHAPTER FIFTEEN

Miren

There is only darkness in his eyes. I thought I could talk to him, calm him down. I knew I should have come clean ages ago, but it's been nice to have a place to belong. Just for a while. However, it seems my time has run out. The luck I had been riding has come to an end.

"So what brought you to his house?" His words are a whisper dripping in poison as they touch my lips. When I don't reply, he wraps a hand around my neck. The pressure on my throat is intense, and he digs his fingers into the sides, stealing my air. "I have no qualms making you cry, wee fox," he tells me. "Get up," he orders, and even if I wanted to refuse him, I can't because he lifts me with ease. The grip he has on me is strong, harsh. If he were to press any harder, I'd most probably pass out.

"I-I was kidnapped," I choke out slowly. My voice raspy as I voice my response.

Monster tips his head to the side as he walks us back until I hit the wall with a soft thud. "And I'm meant to believe that?"

The sneer on his face makes my heart riot against my ribs. My lungs are struggling, and my head feels light, as if there are bubbles floating in there. Gently, I place my hands on his forearm and feel the corded muscles as they tense at my touch.

"Yes," I rasp. "I-I wouldn't lie."

"Oh?" He smirks, and I realise I kind of did. I omitted information. It isn't the same as lying. "You are a liar." His sneer is venomous.

I shouldn't be saddened by his anger at me, but for some reason, I am. The kiss we shared was nothing more than me thanking him for his help, but deep down, I know it was more. I felt it. There was a current of need that had coursed through me the moment my lips touched his cheek. The short stubble tickling my lips, and last night in bed, I replayed the moment in my head, over and over again. The memory of his tongue tasting my lips sent me over the edge.

There's a long, silent moment where he just stares at me. I dart my tongue out to lick my lips, and those dark orbs drop to my mouth. Heat flickers in his stare. Then the hand he'd been holding me with snakes around to my hair, and he fists the locks before tugging my head back. My neck exposed, Monster leans in and slowly inhales, as if he's committing my scent to memory.

"You're a distraction," he tells me. The words slam into me. I should have been upfront, but I obeyed Father Donahue when he told me to hide the truth. Even though I knew it was wrong, I did it. Whatever happens to me now is in fate's hands. "I don't trust you."

Monster lifts his head from the crook of my neck. His dark eyes simmer. I'm pretty sure he wants to kill me. Perhaps he should, and then this will all be over. Finally.

"Then kill me," I mutter when he only stares at me. "I lied to you, that's true. But I was scared. The truth is, I didn't know who my father was until I was kidnapped by him."

I don't lower my gaze; instead, I hold his hostage

because I know if I were to look away, he'd think I was lying. He needs to see the truth in my eyes.

"Why would a father kidnap his daughter?" Monster asks me, his brows furrowed in confusion.

Even though we're having what I would consider a conversation, he doesn't release his hold on me. And I don't want him to. The realisation that I crave this, I crave him, makes my stomach tumble. I have a crush on the man who wants to hurt me and my family.

"Before I was taken, I overheard my mother talking on the phone," I start, recalling what happened that night. "She told whoever it was, Patrick I assume now, that she won't allow me to see him or visit him. I went up to my room, and when I came down for dinner, she was gone. I was in her office when I found a folder in one of her drawers," I speak, hoping he'll let up, and slowly, ever so fucking slowly, his fingers release my hair.

"What was in the folder?"

"Information about Patrick Bragan and the paternity test confirming my lineage." The memory of what I'd learned is burned into my brain. I can never forget where I come from. A long line of dangerous people.

"And then what?"

"There was someone in my mother's office, and he knocked me out with a cloth wet with chloroform." A shudder wracks through me when I close my eyes and remember that smell. "When I woke, I was in Bragan's house."

"So ye woke up in his house. He kept you there all that time?" Monster asks me before stepping back.

I'm thankful for the reprieve of his anger, but also, I miss him being close. The man is a danger to me, but not to my life. No, the man before me is a danger to my heart. Because when he looks at me, I can tell he's at war with himself. His words, *you're a distraction*, ring in my ears.

"Yes," I tell him. "Patrick questioned me about my mother, her business, and her whereabouts. But I don't know anything. All my life she's always told me she's in banking, and I believed her because I didn't think she had a reason to lie."

He watches me. He doesn't move, and it's almost as if he's not breathing either. The air in the room sparks with volatile energy. I want to run, but I also want to force him to listen and believe me. I don't know why it means so much to me for him to understand, but it does. The man has given me a home when he didn't have to. He's given me a job, something to keep me from having to leave the club. Which also means safety. I'm safe from my father's men, and it seems my mother as well.

"There's somethin' you don't know then," Monster tells me as he steps away and heads over to a filing cabinet against the opposite wall where I'm still standing. He takes pages from a drawer and turns back to me. "These will fill you in." He places the documents on the table.

My feet move slowly. It's like coming face-to-face with a wild animal. No sudden movements to anger it. I take the pages and scan the information. All of them are documents from MI5 as well as Scotland Yard. The name Amanda Walsh is mentioned, which causes my gut to twist in recognition. And then the link makes itself known under the headline—*The search continues for the Head of the Irish mob.*

"I don't understand." I look up to meet Monster's gaze.

"Your Ma," he tells me. "She's the one who runs the organisation. She's the one who ordered a hit on my mother years ago. All these years I thought it was Patrick, but I was wrong." As he tells me this, his eyes turn glossy.

The thought of my mother killing his makes me sick

to my stomach. All these years I believed my mother when she told me what her day was like. How her colleagues knew her. From partnerships around the world, to day to day running of a finance company. Nothing ever stuck out at me as strange. Not even now when I think about it.

But, there's no doubt, the documents in my hand confirm she is the dangerous one.

"What about Patrick? If she's running things, why is he included in this?"

"When she took over, yer da became second-in-command. If she were dead," Monster tells me, "then he would inherit the whole feckin' lot of it."

I drop my gaze to the pages in my hand, and I notice I'm trembling. I was in his house; he could have so easily killed me. All those questions he asked now make sense. The money, the partners, everything. Even our trips we took. "I don't understand why he waited so long, though. I mean, we lived in London my whole life. If he truly wanted to find her, he could have."

And it's true. We weren't far away. Being in Northern Ireland, we're only a ferry trip or flight away. It would not have stopped him if he was so adamant to step up as head of the organisation.

"It seems that was all yer grandda's doin'."

Monster hands me another document that he pulled from the same drawer. It's a copy of my grandfather's will. I never met the man. He died before I was born. But it's clear in black and white, if something happened to my mother, the organisation would automatically fall under my name. There'd be a custodian who would step in if I were under the age of twenty-one, and once I come of age, I would automatically be forced into the head seat. So, no matter the outcome, I would always be the leader, and not Patrick. Either way, he's lost out, and he's angry. I was in his home, he could have killed me. *Why didn't he?*

"I don't understand. My grandfather should have foreseen that Patrick would want to kill me. It didn't matter how old I was. He had me in his home, right under his thumb, and yet all he did was question me."

"Aye, he coulda killed ye, but I have a feelin' the man had a heart when he saw ye. However, yer mother forced his hand. There was a rumour going around the organisations that she was to fake her own death. I think she chose to trust the wrong people, men who were loyal to yer da, and they told him. Which brings us to the here and now. Yer ma is in America somewhere. I have a feeling she didn't tell ye because she knew yer da would torture the truth out of ye."

"I didn't know any of this," I say as the betrayal hits me. All my life has been a lie. The woman I loved and trusted lied to me. I may have kept my real name from Monster, from the club, but I never once lied to them. All the things I told them have been me. "I..." Shaking my head, I sink into the chair and allow my face to fall into my hands. It's as if waves are crashing over me, and I want to sink into them. I want to drown. It's the only way this will stop.

"Look at me," Monster says in a deep, commanding tone. He doesn't speak until I obey him. "This is shite," he says. "But you're stronger than that. Aren't ye?"

"I don't know." The brutal honesty makes my throat burn. The tears I'd been fighting take over, and I allow them to fall. "I'm sorry I didn't tell you who I was. Who I am. But I didn't know either. It seems everything I knew about my family, my life, it's all been a lie."

Monster rounds the table and stops right beside me. He offers me his hand, which after a moment of uncertainty I accept. And then he pulls me to my feet. Moments ago, this man was going to kill me. He wanted to hurt me. And now, he's cupping my face in his large, strong hand so gently I tremble.

"I can tell you're a strong woman, Miren." His words offer the sweetest comfort. "Ye should fight back, show them what ye're made of." This time, he chuckles. "Ye can fight me well enough." His words make me smile. I can't stop it. And he offers me a grin. The anger that was so clear in his gaze earlier is gone, and I'm met with the man under the Monster façade. He's not as bad as he thinks he is. If he was, if he truly was a monster, he'd have killed me.

"So, he's going to come for me."

"Aye," Monster says. "I don't believe he died in that explosion, and I am convinced he killed Donahue." There's a hint of sadness in his eyes. He was obviously close to the priest. My heart aches for the lives lost because of my father. Because of my mother.

"I'm sorry," I whisper as his thumb swipes along my lower lip. "For your mother, and for Father Donahue," I tell him.

Those dark eyes, the ones that hold so much pain, lift to mine. He's not told me much about himself, but I know he's good. He has a heart of gold, and he cares. Even though he tries to act as if he doesn't, I can see how he is with the men he considers family. The women too. All the girls at the club speak highly of him.

"It's not ye who pulled the trigger," he says then. "But those who did, those who ordered the kill, they will pay."

I should be scared. But the man before me, the one promising to kill both my parents, doesn't scare me. Instead, he has my respect. I don't agree with violence, but I most certainly do not think innocent people should be hurt. And both the priest and Monster's mother were innocent.

"What is your name?" I don't know why the words slip from my tongue now, but they do.

His lips turn into a smile. "That's what ye want to know?"

"Aye," I answer in an attempt to mimic his accent, which makes him chuckle.

"Cathal," he tells me. "But nobody calls me that anymore. I haven't been that man in a very long time, wee fox."

Tipping my head to the side, I look up at him and ask, "And why do you call me a fox?"

This time, he laughs out loud. The rumble vibrates through his chest. I enjoy the sound of it, and I want to hear him laugh all the time.

"Because ye're a wily, wee thing," he tells me. "Hidin' secrets and such from us. Any farmer will tell ye, never trust havin' foxes around. They'll steal yer chickens and make off with them."

"I don't steal chickens," I throw back, but I don't

stop smiling.

"Aye, but ye're stealin' somethin' much more precious." He doesn't tell me what because he releases me and steps back. "Let's go. We're goin' ta need to talk to the boyos. They need to know everythin' you've just told me."

And I realise I won't be getting any answers from him about what he meant. Not today anyway. So, instead of fighting him on it, I appease and follow him out the door and into the main area of the clubhouse.

It's time to come clean.

Time to face the consequences.

CHAPTER SIXTEEN

Monster

The warehouse is cold and dank. Winter has hit us with an icy, rainy feckin' day. Miren is shaking, but I refrain from offering her a jacket. I still can't trust her. The man who's bound on the chair before me is one of her father's soldiers.

I should have been at the feckin' harbour right now bringin' in the shipment, but I had to trust my VP to handle it. My message to Judah was received. He assured me he'd be there and oversee any implications that might crop up. There are too many feckin' fires to put out right now, and I don't like it.

When we're stretched thin like this, it can be dangerous. I stop in front of our man who's looking between us as if he's goin' ta shit himself. His glare lands on the girl, on Miren, and he seems to sober up.

"You," he sneers as he looks her up and down. "You're meant to be on our side. What you doing with these biker bastards?"

I rear back, and my fist makes contact with his face, causin' him to howl in pain. I don't allow any feckin' arsehole to talk about my club like that. No matter we are the feckin' Royal Bastards.

"Where are Patrick and Sinéad?" I ask him, gripping his cheeks and turning his attention on me.

The questions about Miren will come later. The important information I need right now is where the feck those two are. I know Patrick isn't dead. Evil doesn't die—it hides. It lies in wait until you let your guard down.

When he doesn't answer, I nod for my implements to be brought over. The sleek metal tray is carried by one of the prospects. Out of all of them, he's shown the most promise of bein' patched in. The boy is only twenty, but he has a strong stomach, which is what we need here.

I grab one of the heavy metal hooks. It's big enough to cause enough damage to get a man talkin'. But it's small enough to fit into the eyelid.

"What the fuck are you doing with that?" our man asks.

With a grin, I grip his eyelashes, and I tug. When the lid comes away from the eye, I move quickly. The beggin' and pleadin' starts, but I ignore the request for mercy. A gasp comes from behind me, and her gentle sound, which I want to hear the moment I slide into her cunt, is like music to my ears. If Miren thinks this is bad, though, she'll be more shocked at what I have in store for her da and that bitch mother of hers.

I've never in my life hurt a woman. Never wanted to. Until I learned of the real reason my ma is dead. The hit was ordered by Sinéad. And even though I haven't yet heard her reasons, I won't give a shite about why.

The blood that seeps down this arsehole's face is like a feckin' waterfall of red.

"Please, you're a fucking monster," he cries out in agony.

Offering him a smile, I say, "Aye, tell me somethin' I don't know." I straighten up, still holding onto the metal that's pierced through the soft skin of his eyelid. "Where is yer boss?" I hiss, low and feral. I'm tense, my shoulders are tight, and my hand is fisted at my side, needing to hurt someone, something.

"If you think I'm going to talk, you're sorely mistaken," he tells me. "You can do anything you want. I'm not fucking talking."

I have never been one to shy away from an invitation like that. With a smile, I reach for the black gloves and slide them on while keeping my focus on the man before me. I pick up the next implement—a long, thick needle.

"I've always enjoyed bein' creative when it comes to talkin' to arseholes like yourself," I murmur as I lean forward, one hand on the arm of the chair, the other holding onto the needle. "Hammer," I call to the new prospect. I need his assistance. "Why don't we help our guest out of his trousers and pants?"

Once I can grab his flaccid dick with my gloved hand, I hold the small shaft and smile at the fecker before I press the long steel blade into the slit of his cock. His cries of pure agony fill the room.

"Ye know, some men find this a turn-on," I tell him calmly as if I'm tellin' him the weather forecast.

"Fuck, stop. Please stop," he begs when the sleek silver has almost penetrated him fully. "I-I don't know where they are. Both of them. Please. I don't, I really don't." His brow is dripping with sweat, and there's blood trickling from his cock. Without warning, I pull the needle out, which earns me a cry of utter distress.

"Clean this up," I tell the men before I pull the gloves off and take one last look at the bastard. I slam my fist into his mouth, which paints my hand in his blood. "You'll died today." I turn and walk away with Miren following close behind me.

"Feck!" My voice booms as I walk into the small office in the corner of the warehouse. I'm sure everyone can hear us. I don't give a shite. They can listen all they want because they know who I am. Not finding Sinéad and Patrick is frustrating. It's feckin' with my head.

I glance at Miren, and as much as I want her dead, I can't feckin' bring myself to hurt her. I've learned her real name. She's the one hiding in plain sight, but yet she's nothing like her father. I'm torn between wanting to kill her and wanting to kiss her. "You can't stay here. You can't be near me. There's no way this is goin' ta work. Why are you feckin' with my head?"

She shakes her head sadly. Her eyes shimmer with unshed tears as she stares up at me. "I've never felt this way before. Never wanted to be close to someone as much as I do with you. And I know it's wrong."

Her confession is enough to have my blood boilin'

in my veins.

She can't want me.

She can't feel anythin' for me.

I spent my life hiding from emotions I know will end up killin' me, and the path to love, to allowin' my heart to feel, is one of those. I haven't said those words to anyone since I said goodbye to Ma.

I push her against the wall, pinning her between the cold concrete and my body. I'm drenched in another man's blood, but I don't care. I reach up and swipe her cheek with my thumb. Her porcelain flesh is now smeared with crimson.

"You're a liar," I tell her as I lower my mouth to hers. But I don't kiss her, I merely tease my tongue over her lips, much like I did before. "You may taste like heaven, but you're the ultimate sin," I whisper. My words hurt her because she flinches at my insult. "You're the living incarnation of him. Your blood is his blood. What makes you different? What makes you someone I should save?"

Miren blinks as she stares at me. The tears trickle down her cheeks, and I know I've hit her hard. Not with my hands, but with my words. She knows her father is the devil in-fecking-carnate. But you can't change blood. It runs through yer veins until there's nothing left but the knowing you're forever connected to them.

"I'm… I'm…"

"Sorry?" I arch a brow at her. I don't want her apology. I need her father to feckin' pay for what he's done. Now that we know he's alive, we will find the bastard. The problem is, she knows her ma is the ringleader. Her mother oversees the feckin' Irish mob. A woman who has no qualms about killin' innocent people. She's done it once, and I know she'll do it again. There's no way she's getting her princess back. I wanted to get revenge, and the best way to do that is to keep the pretty wee fox to myself. The monster will devour the precious girl until there's nothing left.

"I don't believe anyone should pay for the sins of another," Miren tells me. "Yes, his blood runs through my veins, but my soul is nothing like his."

She lowers her teary gaze, and I want to lift her chin just to see those strange-coloured eyes again. I've never seen anything like them. The soft shade of blue reminds me of the sky on a cool winter's day. Almost white. I never met anyone who looks as ethereal. Long, dark hair hangs down her back, and I can't stop my gaze from drinkin' in her soft curves. Wide hips with a gentle slope that offers the view of her arse I'm dyin' to spank.

Anger turns to lust.

The feckin' roller coaster this girl has me on is drainin'. "You need to tell us everythin', and I mean it, Miren. Yer da is still alive, and I ain't stoppin' until I've got his blood on my hands."

"Is that going to bring your mother back?" Her voice is tender, gentle. She's not tryin' to hurt me. She's genuinely askin'.

"No, but it can stop him from hurtin' others, from taking loved ones from families." When I first started my crusade, I was focused on revenge. I wanted to make sure I watched the man die, but now, I want nothing more than to keep others safe from his brutal violence.

"The whole idea of an eye for an eye is wrong," Miren tells me.

I know this, but I don't acknowledge it. I don't allow her to see what I'm feelin'. Showing emotions only gets you hurt. I learned the lesson from watchin' others.

I push away from the wall and head out of the room. The warehouse has grounds that rival even the clubhouse gardens. Da made sure he lived in luxury and tortured in privacy. There's feck all around here. Nobody can hear the screams.

But our home, the clubhouse, was special to him. He

believed that even though we were a motorcycle club we didn't have to live in a dive. He wanted to ensure the house, the grounds, the place where the brothers felt at home was beautiful. He wanted us to all feel safe.

Miren follows me outside. Her presence is like a shadow, as if she's attached to me somehow, and I doubt I'll ever rip her from me. We stand in silence beside each other. When I'm around others, I'm tense. The brothers know this, and they give me space when I need it, but Miren has no clue. However, her standing next to me doesn't twist my gut into knots. Her soft fragrance of cherries calms my thudding pulse.

She doesn't say anything for a long while, and I'm thankful for the quiet. Even though the noise from the bar filters out to us, it's the silence between us that feels as if it's holding me in a gentle grip.

"Love is a blade," I tell her without looking at her. "It cuts you the moment you relinquish control to it." It's an idea, a thought I've had for so long it feels normal to tell it to her. I've never mentioned it to any of the brothers. They may know me well, but there are still secrets of mine I hold close to my chest. And it's taken a wee lassie to dig up the dirt.

"It's sad you think so," she tells me. "You're afraid of it," Miren muses with a softness to her voice.

"Nothing scares me," I tell her, shrugging it off as if it's nothin', but if I had to be honest, Miren is right. The fear of loving and losing has always kept those emotions at bay.

She steps down onto the grass before slipping off her sandals and pressin' her toes into the ground. I watch as she laughs when they sink into the wetness, and when she looks up, there's an innocence to her I never noticed before.

The sky opens up, and the clouds that have been hangin' overhead burst, soaking Miren. Her long, dark hair is matted to her, and the dress she's wearing hugs every feckin' perfect curve of her body. The softness of her has me hardening. Seein' her nipples poke through the material has my thoughts delving into the darkness. I want to devour every inch of her.

"Ye like the rain?" I muse.

She looks over at me, and for the first time since I saw her at that mansion as the concrete and bricks crumbled to the ground, I see happiness in her eyes. There's no stress, no pain or heartache. It's as if the rain has washed away every worry she carries with her.

And I find myself wanting to feel it too. My feet carry me off the veranda and onto the grass. My boots squelch in the wetness as I make my way towards her.

She doesn't run. Most women would. They'd see me comin' and cross the street so they're on the opposite side. Far away from me. A biker who has blood on his hands.

"Close your eyes," she tells me, and I do. Her hands cup my cheeks. Most women wouldn't get this close to me. In the past, when I fucked, they'd be bent over, takin' me from behind. But I allow Miren to place her hands on me.

The droplets are large, and they hit me in ways a shower couldn't. It's the coolness of them that makes the knots in my muscles ease. Miren doesn't release me. When I open my eyes again, she's staring straight at me. I shrug off my cut and wrap it around her shoulders.

When she looks at me with confusion, I say, "Don't need the brothers in there seein' those pretty little nipples. I don't want any of them lookin' at ye."

Her blush is obvious as her cheeks turn a deep red. I take a step closer to her, our bodies flush under the rain. I reach for her arse and grip both cheeks in my hands and lift her against me. I don't give a shite if they're watching inside, I lean in to steal her lips.

A soft moan falls from Miren, and I swallow it back as our tongues stroke along each other. The movement sends desire rippling through me. I want to press her against a wall, to rip her dress off and claim her right here. It's been a long time coming since she walked into my life, into my home. But I won't do it where all can see.

"Monster," Míren moans my name, her lips whispering along mine. "I... I don't know—" Her voice breaks, and I capture her mouth again. I don't want her to tell me she doesn't want this. One more taste, just one more, and I'll let her go. Once I pull away, I lower her to her feet and step back. The rain hasn't stopped, it hasn't even let up, but when she looks up at me, I don't see guilt in her eyes. "I'm not ready for this. Not yet. Can we? Can we just talk for a while?"

Confusion settles in my chest. "Aye, of course. What did ye think? I was goin' ta walk off and leave ye here if ye weren't into it?"

She laughs. It's a soft, melodic sound, and for a moment, she looks at me as if I'm strange. "No. I just know that men get angry when they're turned down. And I'm not turning you down. I just..." She waves her hand in the air and looks away. "Need some time."

Surprise bursts in my mind, and my mouth pops open in shock. "Listen to me, and listen good," I say. "I'm not a feckin' arsehole. When you're ready for this, I'll take ye up to that bedroom and make ye scream my feckin' name. But until then, we will do as you wish. Talk? Aye, I can talk fer days."

This makes her giggle. A gentle trickle of a sound. Like water on pebbles, calming and relaxing. I want her to do it all feckin' day. I still can't believe she thought I'd be angry about not getting sex. It's bafflin' that any man would make a woman feel like that.

I look her dead in the eye and say, "I may be a biker, but I'm a feckin' gentleman."

"Well," she says and pauses for a moment. "I think we should sit down and talk. Perhaps you can tell me about growing up in Belfast, and I'll tell you about London. They're very different cities."

I smile as we head down to the benches and take a seat. I haven't actually spent time here since I took over. Usually, I'm in the office workin' or I'm in my bedroom.

"Belfast is one of those cities that settles in yer bones. It's always had turmoil and violence attached to it. But growin' up here, I feckin' loved it. There's an energy here you can't find anywhere else in the world. But I guess you'd say that about London as well."

She smiles and nods. "Yeah, London is an entity. I suppose most cities are. I think it's the people who bring a city to life. It's their excitement and love for a place that makes it what it is."

"You're insightful for a wee fox that's still so young," I remark.

"Well, I studied the human mind, and I think that's given me a deeper insight into people and their thinking. It's definitely something I've found a passion for." When she talks about her studies, I can see the excitement that shines in her eyes, in her expression.

And I realise watching her, I want to see that look on her face all the time.

"Then you'll have to find a practice once this is all over," I tell her.

But as the words come out, I realise it's not the happiest of thoughts. I know she has to go sometime. Once her folks are in prison or dead, I don't mind either, she's going to go on with her life. It's the reason I've fought this attraction. This requirement to protect her won't be there forever.

She has a life outside the motorcycle club. I'm pretty sure she has friends and colleagues who want to see her again. And I can't hold her back from that. No matter how much I want her to stay. Havin' her close is somethin' special, but one day, like everyone in my life, she'll leave.

And I'm going to have to say goodbye again.

"I might," she answers me suddenly, dragging me away from my dark thoughts. "But I can't tell the future, so who knows what's going to happen? There are so many factors that could change the path of anyone's life."

"You have to go," I tell her. "There's no life here for you. Not for the kind of work you're goin' ta do. Helpin' people is important."

"You want me to go?" Her eyes penetrate right through me.

I don't respond, because I'm not sure how to. If I said no, she'd think there's more here, but also, I don't know if I can get attached to someone who can up and leave at any time.

A moment passes, and Miren pushes to her feet. It's dark, and I can't see if she's angry.

"Where are you goin'?"

"To sleep." Her voice is tight with emotion, and I watch her leave.

I should go after her, but I don't because I have no claim on her. Aye, we coulda fucked tonight, but it didn't happen. Probably for the best.

A flick of a lighter catches my attention. Sully saunters over to where I am and leans against the wall. "Big mistake, brother," he tells me. "Big fuckin' mistake." I don't argue with him, because for the first time in my life, I can't deny it.

CHAPTER SEVENTEEN

Miren

The long, heavy wooden dinner table is filled with the brothers, the Bastards, and a few of the girls who work in the club. Callia is seated beside me, and I know she's going to ask about Monster's fascination with me. He's been following me around since he found out the truth. Watching me when I'm at work, walking me back to my room. He hasn't once touched me or tried to kiss me again, but his attention is focused. So much so that the guys have been whispering about him finally claiming someone.

I'm not sure how I feel about it. My focus is still on finding my mother and Patrick. He will always be a monster in my eyes, more so than the man who took me in when I needed protection. The sadness that does come over me when I think about what my mum did still eats away at me. The guilt of her actions has chosen to take its ire out on me.

As much as I want to be normal, to forget about the past, I can't. I glance around the table, and when my gaze locks on Monster, he's staring. Much like he's done since the first day I saw him. He doesn't smile or offer a hint as to what he's thinking.

"Are you two finally getting some?" Callia whispers in my ear, causing my cheeks to heat, and I force myself to look away from him.

"No," I tell her. "What are you even talking about?"

"Oh please," she hisses. "I can see the sexual tension between the two of ye. It's so obvious. I'm pretty sure if you were to tell him you want to go upstairs right now, the man would drag you up there. Or he'd most probably bend you over this table and show everyone you're his."

"Calli!" I gasp out loud, causing a few of the guys to turn to us. Rebel looks over, his gaze narrowing on us.

"Aye, he's an eejit if he doesn't do something soon."

She winks at me, accompanied by a soft giggle.

As much as she's embarrassing me right now, I can't help but smile. It feels good to be welcomed. Even after the lads found out who I really am. I was convinced I would be sent packing, or buried six feet under, but they've given me the benefit of the doubt. There's no way I intend on breaking my promise to stand by them when it comes down to it. It was an easy decision.

The music is turned up, and the rest of the family seated around the table shout and cheer. The beer is flowing freely, and so is the whisky. Callia pulls me from the chair, and we hold hands as we move to the middle of the room. It's enormous, with a pool table off to one side and a jukebox on the other. A curved bar sits in the corner, opposite the entrance. A couple of the prospects are serving drinks, while a handful of the guys are playing darts. The dim lighting offers enough illumination to make it feel homely, almost magical.

With the heavy rain outside, it's warm indoors. The song changes, and 'Do You Remember' by Jarryd James fills the room. Callia and I start dancing with each other—slowly, sensually. I wonder if she's trying to get Rebel jealous, or perhaps tease him. I'm not sure, but I can feel a pair of eyes burning into my back. When I spin around, I find Monster watching me.

Callia's hands grip my hips, and we both twist as we lower into a crouch before rising again. I wouldn't work in the club, but I feel comfortable here with the brand-new family I've found.

I turn to face her again as the next song comes on. 'Drive You Insane' by Daniel Di Angelo. We're dancing together, giggling like schoolgirls when suddenly I'm ripped from Callia's arms and dragged out of the room by the big, strong hands of the President of the Royal Bastards MC. When we reach the long, empty hallway, he spins on his heel, ensuring my back is right up against the smooth, cold wall.

"Are ye tryin' ta feck with my head?" His question is sneered, but the look in his eyes is pure lust. Dark, seductive, and alluring. The man is the epitome of a monster right now. Ready to devour its prey. And I'm caught in the line of fire.

"What do you mean?"

"Don't feckin' ask me stupid shite. You and Callia dancin' around like ye need the cash."

My hand makes contact with his face before he has time to grab me. But he slams both his palms against the wall beside my head, causing me to wince. I'm surprised the concrete hasn't given way with the strength he put into the movement.

"Fuck you," I spit out as anger overtakes me. I'm not scared of him. I haven't been, even when I was about to die by his hand. I'm not some little girl he can push around and expect me to cower. "I can dance with whoever I want to dance with. If I picked out one of the men, what would you have done then?"

"Kill ye both," he responds without blinking. And I realise he's dead fucking serious. He would as well.

"I don't belong to anyone."

"Like feck ye do." His voice is getting louder with every moment that passes. "You're mine."

I fold my arms across my chest, which only makes them brush against the hard, muscled torso holding me hostage. Monster's gaze falls to my chest, and the lust I saw earlier only seems to burn brighter when he takes in my low-cut top.

"Am I?"

"You've walked in here, and you've fecked with my head," he tells me earnestly. "Since I saw you standin' beside Donahue, I've wanted nothin' more than to taste ye, every feckin' inch of ye. That night when I walked ye to yer room, that small taste wasn't enough. It will never be enough."

Frustration blooms in my gut. I didn't think he felt anything until that night. Before that, I was convinced he hated me. And then when he found out who I really was, it was evident that he may feel the attraction, but he fought it. And he continues to fight it.

"Then show me!"

"You're too feckin' sweet! There's not a chance in hell I can allow you to want a monster!"

His voice booms against the walls. I'm pretty sure every person in the room next door has heard him. He doesn't at all seem concerned, though. His eyes burn right through me.

"You don't *allow* me to do anything," I bite out. "I'm my own person. I don't take orders, and I don't cower to any fucking person." I push against his chest, but he doesn't move. He's far too strong, and I have nothing compared to the weight of him. "Let me go."

That's when he grips my arms, his hands holding onto me as if I'm a buoy out at sea, a lifeline. Monster glares at me, the rage filling the space between us. But then, his eyes glint at something else. They soften. It's miniscule, but I see it.

His voice breaks when he admits, "I can't."

Before I can say anything more, he leans in and steals my lips with his. The gentleness in his kiss doesn't last long before his hands grip my arse, and he lifts me against him. My legs wrap around his waist, and he presses me between the wall and his hard frame.

The possessiveness in Monster's touch makes my stomach tumble and my heart leap into my throat. His tongue snakes between my lips and dances along mine. Heat courses through my veins, and a soft moan vibrates in my throat when I feel his erection against my core. We fit. It's as if we're two magnets that have slowly been forced together and suddenly snap into place.

I didn't expect to feel like this. To ache for someone like I do him. Even with his mouth on mine, stealing my breath, and his hands holding me, I can't stop wanting to get closer. I want every part of me to be attached to every part of him.

The music next door fades into nothing, and my focus is now solely on the man who's devouring me whole. The Monster was never hidden under my bed— he was right in front of me, hungry, feral, and filled with pain. And I want nothing more than to feed him, to heal him, to make him feel something other than the need for vengeance.

When he finally pulls away and breaks the kiss, we're both breathing heavily. My chest rises and falls, brushing against his. The motion only serves to make my nipples harden. They're sensitive with every movement. The tremble that shoots through my body has him smirking.

"If I were to touch you right now," Cathal whispers, "will I find that pretty cunt wet for me?" His eyes turn darker as if he's no longer human, but completely and utterly taken over by animalistic lust.

I tip my head to the side and smile. "Why don't you take me to my room and find out?"

He doesn't need a second invitation, because he carries me up the stairs and down the hall until we reach the bedroom I'd been given. I open the door, and Cathal kicks it closed behind us. He heads straight for the bed and drops me on the mattress.

I lie back, my gaze never leaving his as he slowly shrugs off his cut. Then, with fire dancing in his dark eyes, he reaches for his T-shirt and pulls it over his head. It falls to the floor, and I finally get my first look at him.

The man is huge. I mean, his shoulders are wide. Muscles seem to come alive each time he moves. They tense and release as he unbuckles his belt. A whoosh of leather through the denim loops are the only sound in the room.

"Like the view, wee fox?" he asks me. The satisfaction in his tone makes me smile. He knows I'm enjoying looking at him.

"Don't flatter yourself," I tell him before rolling over and looking out the window instead.

It's a mistake because his hand lands on my arse cheek with a loud swat, which has me squealing and trying to get away. But he's fast. He grips my ankles and drags me down the bed until I'm bent over in front of him.

"Going somewhere, sweetheart?" The gravel in his tone rumbles over the words, sending a shiver down my spine.

Another swat lands on my arse, and I'm once again trying to claw my way up the bed, but it's no use. The leggings I was wearing slowly slip over my bum as Cathal tugs them down to my ankles, and soon, I'm only in a pair of panties. He leaves the leggings where they are, which ensures I'm not able to run away. Then my underwear is pushed to the side.

I glance over my shoulder and watch as he runs his fingers up my inner thighs. He'll soon find out I'm drenched. I'm more turned on than I've ever been. And it's all because of a monster.

"Mm," he murmurs when his index finger finds my slit. "Just like I thought." I watch as he brings the digit to his lips and slowly tastes me with those dark orbs pinned on mine.

"Cathal," I murmur, and he glances up. "Please," I beg. I want more, so much fucking more, but I'm shy to ask for it.

Fighting with him is easy, I can do that without a second thought, but this, this is different.

"Tell me, wee fox," he coaxes. "Tell me what you need."

He dips a finger between my legs once more, and my eyes roll back as pleasure warms its way through my body. Every nerve ending is alight with electricity as he gently traces his finger over my wetness. Again and again. When he stops, he adds a second digit before dipping them inside me, which has me whimpering.

My hips lift off the bed, only to have him chuckle, but he swats my arse again as he circles my clit with his wet fingers. My toes curl in my trainers as the expert touch of the monster behind me sends me into orbit.

Mewls and moans escape my lips, and I'm so close to my release, nearing the edge, I can practically taste the explosion of pleasure. But then he pulls away, and I can't stop the whine of frustration from falling easily from my mouth.

"Do ye really think I'm goin' ta have ye comin' while my dick ain't inside ye?" He's not joking. Far from it.

He lifts my ankles and spins me over. I'm on my back, looking up at the beauty of him. He doesn't say a word as he takes off my shoes, then my socks and leggings. "Off wit ye wee tank top," he orders. "I want to see all of ye."

I obey. It's the only thing I can do because I want this. I want him. I unclasp my bra and allow it to fall from my shoulders. If I thought he was feral before, he's practically salivating at the sight of me now. My cheeks heat with embarrassment because a man has never looked at me like this. If I had to be honest, my ex-boyfriend never trailed his gaze over me as if I were the most beautiful thing he'd ever seen.

"You're feckin' beautiful," Cathal says, his gaze taking in every inch of me.

His hands move to the button of his jeans, then the zip hisses as he slowly pushes it down. He's teasing. When his jeans lower to his thighs, I must force myself to not have my mouth drop open. Every part of him is toned with corded muscle. And then there's the thickness against the tight fabric of his underwear.

"C'mere to me, wee fox. Show me how much ye want me."

I sit up and hook my fingers in the waistband before tugging the briefs down. His cock, thick and hard, juts out. Leaning in, I lap at the wet tip, and his arousal paints my tongue. He's salty, delicious, and I want more. Wrapping my lips around the tip, I slide my mouth down the length until it hits the back of my throat.

"Feck!" The grunt of pleasure that escapes him makes me smile. I continue my ministrations, sending a vibration of need coursing down his cock when I hum. "You're goin' ta have ta stop that," he tells me. I release him from my mouth and scoot back on the bed until he drops to his knees and spreads my thighs. With one finger, he shifts my panties to the side and then his wet, warm tongue is on my pussy.

He laps at me like a starving man. Gently, he circles my clit with one finger while another dips inside me as he sucks on me. He devours me until my legs are shaking and my toes have curled into the sheet.

"Cathal," I call out when I'm nearing the edge.

But this time, he doesn't stop. He adds a second and then a third finger inside me. He pumps them faster and faster until I'm screaming out his name. I don't care who hears me. I'm lost in pleasure as I tip over the edge.

Short moments pass, and I come down from the high. I open my eyes to find Monster nestled between my legs. He fits there perfectly, like he was made to be there. His erection nudges at me, and I nod. "Please."

Ever so slowly, he teases his way into me. He presses his lips to mine, and I taste myself on his tongue. With every inch he fills me with, the more I dig my nails into his shoulders.

My back arches from the bed by the time he's fully seated. I'm filled, stretched, and it feels amazing. Those dark eyes are on me, keeping me in the present moment. I don't want to be anywhere else but here with him.

"You're feckin' stunnin'." There's a gentle affection in his words. "Ye fit around me like a feckin' glove, sweet girl." His hips move slowly, pulling out, and thrusting back in.

"Cathal, please, I..." There are no words. I can't come up with the words to ask him for what I want or need. I'm lost to the pleasure of him. And I don't ever want to be anywhere else.

CHAPTER EIGHTEEN

Monster

"Tell me, wee fox," I coax as I fuck her, my cock thick and aching as her body pulses around me. The warmth of her coats my shaft when I move, her body accepts mine when I thrust deep. This has to be a once-off. I can't taint her with my need for vengeance. I've already told her I want to kill her folks. I'm surprised she's still here and hasn't run off.

"I need you to fuck me," Miren whispers as she cups my face in her hands and holds me steady.

I want to turn away because when I look at her, I

realise all the bad things I've done have made sure I'm tortured like this. With her. There have been secrets between us, but now they're out in the open, I want to know more. I want to dig into her mind and uncover all she keeps in that pretty head. Those strange-coloured eyes stare at me, waiting for my response. I pull out and slam back in, knocking the breath from her lungs.

"This world is not for you," I tell her as I claim her. "Everyone who had an ounce of good in them is dead. Happiness doesn't flourish here, wee fox. We live in darkness. We revel in it," I say as I stare down at the beauty below me.

"You don't scare me, Monster," she says before wrapping her legs around my waist. She holds onto me as if I were a lifeline. As if she were drownin' and I were the only thing that can keep her afloat. "None of you do. I wouldn't be here if you did."

All these years I've been alone. It suited me fine. I also learned never to allow anyone in, not into the depths of my soul where if they leave, it will hurt. Far too feckin' much.

"I am not good for you," I finally answer as I slam into her once more. I love how her tits move when I fuck her. When I fill her with every feckin' inch of me.

"Do you want me to leave? Even with your dick

inside me, you're telling me you don't want me?" In her eyes, I find annoyance. She has no feckin' reason to trust me, the same as I have no way of trustin' her.

"Aye," I finally respond after a moment.

"Then let me go," she hisses as she tries to wiggle away from me. *Not a fucking chance.* I grip her wrists and pin them beside her. Then I lose all feckin' control.

"Like feck you'll leave," I promise and thrust deep. Over and over again.

My mouth captures her nipple, and I bite down hard until she cries out. Her cunt tightens around me, pulsing wildly around my cock. I suck the hardened bud and lave against it with my tongue, soothing the pain I've just inflicted. She still fights me, even though I feel the flutters of her walls. I reach up with one hand and grip her throat before slamming into her as deep as I can go. I don't relent when I capture her other nipple and bite down. That, sends her over the edge. Her cunt tightens around my cock like a vice.

She's *the* forbidden feckin' fruit. I want nothing more than to bruise every inch of her. Then peel back her layers before gorgin' myself until her supple juices are flowing down my chin, over and over again.

It doesn't take long for my orgasm to shudder through me. I pull out quickly, grip my shaft, and I spray my release over her stomach and mound. It looks beautiful on her slightly tanned flesh. I've marked her.

There's no going back now.

"Monster!" Rebel's voice calls from down the hall.

"Feck," I bite out as frustration races through my veins. I look at Miren who's now giggling at my annoyance. "Don't you go anywhere," I tell her as I get up and cover her with a blanket. "Promise me."

"I'm not going anywhere," she assures me.

The coy look on her face makes my dick ache for more, but I need to see what Rebel wants. It's probably important, or he would never have feckin' called me down.

I rush from the room as I shrug on my cut and find the brothers all in the room we use for church. They're seated around the table and look up the moment I walk in. The party has ended. There are no signs of any of the women around.

"What the feck is going on?" I settle in my chair and look at my VP.

The concern in his expression has me on edge. I don't like not knowing what's happening, especially when it comes to my men.

"Tye got some new info," Rebel tells me before looking at our resident computer genius.

"I got into some emails, a long thread of them," he tells me as he brings over a stack of pages. "But the two pages on the top will explain why we called you down. I didn't think it could wait, and Rebel agreed."

I glance between the men and nod. "Fine." I pick up the first page and scan the details. My stomach drops to my feet when I read the communication. It seems Da wanted Miren's mother dead. Da told Patrick about it, which shocks me because he hated the mob. "Da was workin' with Bragan?"

Tye nods. "I found out when talkin' to our contact at Scotland Yard, ye da was thick in with the Irish mob. This was since before you were born. Patrick wanted rid of Sinéad, and he went to ye da for help. They planned it right down to the hour."

"But Sinéad found out?"

"Aye," Rebel says then. "She ordered a hit on ye ma in retaliation. She wanted to put the fear of God in ye da. But there's more, documents from MI5 confirming ye da was working with them."

"What?" I drop one page and pick up another. My eyes can't read fast enough. There are years' worth of emails, communication between Da and the inspectors and detectives from the agencies in London. "They wanted Patrick. They wanted the whole feckin' Irish mob."

"And ye da agreed. In return, they would provide safety for ye and yer ma." Rebel's words don't take long to sink in. Realisation hits me right in the chest. Da was trying to keep us safe, but he hid the truth from us because he must have known if I were to get taken by the mob, by Sinéad's or Patrick's men, I could have been tortured. It's the only thing that makes sense.

"But instead of protectin' us, he got himself and Ma killed," I bite out before slamming the documents on the table.

Shoving the stack, I create a wave of paper that's scatters across the floor. Pushing the chair back, I rise to full height and place both palms on the table. My gaze meets each man in the room, my focus on them as they look at me. I have to give them the next order, the plan of attack. But I'm too shocked to think straight.

I know Patrick and Sinéad have to pay, there's no doubt about it. But right now, all I can think about is Da doin' somethin' stupid without tellin' us. I spent my life hatin' him. I blamed him for leavin' us alone, and I should blame him for Ma's death. He forced the hand of one of the most dangerous organisations in Ireland.

"Patrick did kill ye da," Rebel says. "We've gone through the paperwork. Tye's been working on it.

There's no doubt about it. Even though Sinéad is the head of the organisation, it was Patrick who pulled the trigger."

Everything seems to crash down around me. I can't find words to ponder what the feck is goin' on. First, I was wrong, then I was right, then wrong again. But now, I'm right, and it was Patrick Bragan.

"When is that feckin' flight comin' in from the across the pond?" I bite out as I pull my mobile phone from my pocket. I shouldn't have it on me in church, but I knew Jameson would be callin' with an update. As if he can hear me, his name flashes on the screen with a call.

"Mate," I answer as I press the device to my ear.

"I have news for you, I don't know if you're going to like it, though," he tells me. Jameson who runs the New Orleans chapter of the Royal Bastards is a brother from over the pond. I'll trust him with my life. "Can you talk?"

"I doubt it can be worse than what I've just learned. Aye, I can talk. What do ye have fer me?" I ask him as I pace the room.

I can feel eyes on me. Every man in this room is tense, watchin' me as if I were a bomb about to go off. I feel like one. If I had to be honest, all I want to do is kill. Red is the only colour I see.

"Sinéad, or Amanda as she's been known here in the States, has just boarded a private jet. We've got the flight schedule from the airstrip. She's headed to London. It's a short stop off for only two hours to refuel, then she's going to New Zealand. From what we can tell, you have eight hours before her plane lands. I'll send you the details."

"The furthest feckin' part of the world she's headin' to. I appreciate yer help on this one," I tell him as I look at Rebel and Tye. Their stares are locked on me. "Thanks, mate," I tell Jameson. "Next time I'm in the South, I'll give you a shout."

"You do that. Drinks are on me," he says with a chuckle.

"Aye, they better feckin' be." Our banter is a bit of fun, and I hang up before looking at my men. "We have to intercept a flight," I tell them. "She's landin' in London. I'll take Rebel and Tye with me. The rest of ye stay here, watch the feckin' compound because I have no doubt Patrick will be comin' for us."

"We'll stay." This comes from Blaze.

Rev nods in agreement. Brute and Banks offer a thumbs up. I know with my brothers here everyone will be safe. Everyone, including Miren. I have a feeling she's going to want to come with us. But I can't let her get into the line of fire. If her mother crosses my path, which she no doubt will, I will kill the bitch.

"I want everyone on high alert. Always keep four prospects at the gates. Any of the women need to leave fer any reason, a brother will escort her where she needs to go. The club will be shut fer a few days. I don't want to put anyone in unnecessary danger."

"What about me?" I snap my gaze to the open door to find Miren standing on the threshold.

I didn't realise the door was open, and now she's overheard what I've said. I don't know how much she's heard, but the look in her eyes tells me it's enough to have her wanting to hitch a ride. Not feckin' happenin'.

"Get things ready," I shout the order at the brothers before I head straight for my girl. I didn't want to think of her in that way, but since I've feckin' marked her, there's no other way to look at this woman now. She's mine.

I grip her arm and drag her through the bar out into the main clubhouse and up the stairs. She's cursin' me as we make our way up to my wing of the house, but I don't give a shite. I'm goin' ta talk now, and she's goin' ta listen.

When we reach my suite, I push open the door and let her enter first. I'm not fighting about this. She's goin' ta have to obey my orders. I want her safe. She may have Bragan's blood racin' through her veins, but she's nothing like him. I can see it now. As much as I wanted to hate her, I can't. I haven't since the moment I laid my eyes on her.

"I'm leavin' tonight," I tell her while I grab a rucksack and start throwing some clothes into it. "You'll stay here with the rest of the brothers."

"I need to see her," Miren tells me, which stops me in my tracks.

I never thought about the fact that it's her mother. I did, but I didn't. When I think about Sinéad, the only thing that comes to mind is that she's a killer. But she is a mother. And I can't stop Miren from wanting to say goodbye.

"You do realise I'm goin' there to kill her." There's no doubt in my tone, in my mind, and in my stance. I don't falter when Miren winces. She must know there's no stopping me. I don't give a shite if it's her ma.

"I understand," Miren says after a long moment of silence. She makes her way over to me and takes my hand. "My family and yours were at war before we came along. Before we knew about it, they'd already made their choices. But I do want to see her. I want to hear why she did what she did."

The genuine shimmer of pain in Miren's eyes makes my chest tighten. Ma always told me one girl, or colleen as she used to call them, would come along and change my views. And it seems Ma was right, as usual. I didn't doubt her, but I was convinced I would be alone because I didn't *want* to fall in love.

I can't say I feel that for Miren, but seein' her strength has my feelin's toward her growin' in a way I have never felt before. "If ye do come with us," I tell her. "I can't promise it's not goin' ta break ye heart."

"I've been heartbroken before," she tells me.

She tips her chin up, the confidence I saw in her since the day we met is unwavering now. If I tell her she can't join us, I'm goin' ta have a fight on my hands. And there's enough violence to go around without another argument.

"Aye," I finally mutter. "Then ye best be ready to leave soon. I don't wait around fer stragglers." I grip her chin between my thumb and forefinger before I lean in and press my lips to hers. "But I will say one thing," I tell her when I pull away from her perfect lips. "The moment I tell ye to leave, you walk away."

"You mean when you finally pull a gun on my mother."

I still don't know how she's okay with this. She's

talking about killing her mother. It's not a walk in the park. I'm a man, a monster who's goin' ta end her ma's life, and she's here kissin' me.

"I think there's somethin' wrong with ye." Perhaps I shouldn't trust her. Maybe she's here because her mother sent her to us. Maybe it's part of an elaborate plan, and I haven't seen the bigger picture.

Miren laughs. "Why?"

I want to tell her my fears. It's stupidity. I don't know this girl. Aye, I've fucked her, but that doesn't mean we're on our way to walkin' down the aisle. I can't let my guard down. It felt good to finally be inside her, but that's all it is.

Nothin' more.

"Get yer stuff," I tell her. "We're leavin' soon."

I allow her to go to her room. And even as I pack my shite, I'm tense. Something doesn't feel right. Everythin' seems too easy. And Miren is too willin' to backstab her ma and da on this.

CHAPTER NINETEEN

Miren

I'm scared.

There isn't anything I've ever backed down from before. Even when I was kidnapped and questioned by Patrick Bragan, I didn't give in. I didn't have anything to offer him, no answers, but I didn't allow him to break me. There were moments I thought he would, but I fought back.

When Monster found out who I really was, I didn't back down. I stood up and waited for death to come. It never did. And now I have a second chance at life.

As I make my way down to the garage, I find the guys waiting on me. Monster is right, I really should stay here, but I must look her in the eye and ask her why she did what she did.

One night, she disappeared, but that was after a lifetime of secrets. My mother doesn't even know if I'm alive or not, and she hasn't tried to get in touch. It doesn't matter what you're going through, your children come first. If I ever had kin, I'd never allow any harm to come to them. They will always be under my protection.

I glance at Cathal as he gives the final orders to the men who are staying behind. I don't listen, because I am too focused on what's to come. This isn't going to be easy by any means. And I know the moment I come face-to-face with her, I'm probably going to allow anger to take over.

Sully brings the van round, and we pile in. He's staying behind but is tasked with driving us to the airport. The flight is short, and I know we'll be there before Mum arrives. It gives me time to think about what I'm going to say.

There are too many things happening all at once. Earlier tonight, I had sex with Cathal. It was the most incredible sexual experience of my life. Not that I have much to go on, but the one guy I've been with never made me feel like Monster does. But, even though there were emotions involved, it doesn't guarantee he'll fall in love with me. I don't even know if I can love him. We're two completely different people from vastly different backgrounds.

Then again, they do say opposites attract. I don't know what's going to happen after this, which forces me to think about what we're about to do. The future feels far away at this moment, and if I were to focus on it, I may not be able to find a way to get the answers I want from my mother.

Sinéad is her real name. Even though I grew up with her, spent every single day with her, I never knew that. All the documents I got to read from Tye were a rude awakening; it was like reading about someone else. A stranger. It's who she is to me now. As much as I loved the woman who raised me, I don't know who she really is.

"Hey," Cathal says. "It's goin' ta be grand."

I nod. "I know. I'm just trying to think of things I want to ask her. It feels as if I've grown up with a stranger. My mother isn't the woman I thought she was. She's a criminal mastermind." A shudder of revulsion courses through me at the thought. Having one of your parents be a criminal is one thing, but for both to be dangerous is different.

"I understand."

"It's a chance now to ask her, to find out about her," Rebel tells me. "Ask her all the things that are running through yer head right now. It's easier, and best to be open, honest. Once you do that, you can hopefully move on sooner."

It's the first time since I came here that he's spoken more than a few words to me, and I offer him a smile. "Thank you." All three men stare at me for a long, silent moment. I don't know what else to say to them, because I don't even know what I want to say. There are no words.

So, we sit in silence until we reach the airstrip. We exit the vehicle and make our way to the plane. Inside, I sit next to Monster who's already got a drink in his hand. I watch as he sips the strong smelling, amber liquid. It's the same as it's always been with him, I can't stop staring. He's breathtakingly gorgeous. Having him beside me has a calming effect, but I know it won't last long.

I lean back and close my eyes as we take off, and I recall the trips Mum took me on. We flew all over the world. There wasn't a city we didn't enjoy visiting.

When she worked, I was studying. But our free time was always spent together. She made sure I was happy. Granted, she bought me things I wanted, but I wasn't spoiled. I would do chores around the house for the items, and I earned my way.

"What are you thinkin'?" Cathal asks me as he leans closer so the others don't hear.

I turn to look at him and smile. "Just thinking about trips I took as a child. Growing up, I went to most cities in Europe, and we went to New Zealand and Australia a few times."

"Ever been to the States?"

"Yeah," I answer with a nod. "A couple of times. But my mother focused mainly on Europe." It's baffling to think all those times she was running a criminal organisation. She was the head of the mob, not just some foot soldier. The thought of it makes me shiver.

"Cold?"

"No." I shake my head. Instead of torturing myself with memories, I close my eyes and try to get some sleep. Soon enough, we'll be in London, and everything that's happened over the past few weeks is going to come to a head. And I have to be ready.

By the time we land, I'm awake again. It was a short but very welcome nap. It's dark out when we disembark, and Cathal greets someone who tells us there's still a few hours before my mother's flight arrives. I really want to go back to my London home and get some of my things, but I also can't leave them here.

I doubt he'll even allow me to go. Cathal made it clear what we are here to do, and if I run off, he may think I'm trying to escape. I've never been a prisoner at the clubhouse, but there was an understanding I had to stay there so they could look after me.

So far, I'm still alive. That's a good thing. We move into the hangar where there are a few cots set up for us to sleep on. I'm exhausted, but the moment I lie down, I'm wide awake. My mind won't shut off. Even when I force myself to close my eyes and block out the light and noise, it doesn't help.

I toss and turn a few times before I hear a squeak on the smooth concrete. Cathal drags his cot over to mine, then he lies down on his mattress and stares up at the roof of the enormous building.

He doesn't speak for a long time, and I'm sure he's fallen asleep. But then he says, "When my ma died, I sat with her body bleeding out in the road. I cried that day. Since then, I haven't shed a tear. She was the only person in my life that I loved. I didn't even consider myself worthy of living when she wasn't."

His sadness seeps into my chest and makes it hard to breathe. I don't know what to say to him. I'm not sure why he's telling me this, but I allow the silence to offer a calm for him.

"She was a good woman." He turns his head to me. "Ye know? Like, deep down, her soul was pure."

When I look at him, I see the love in his eyes. He clearly still feels the pain of her loss. It's been years since she was killed, and yet, the teenage boy who lost his mum is still so evident in the man next to me.

"There aren't many people like that left in the world," I finally speak. "I thought for a long time I was good. I thought my mother was good. It seems I was mistaken."

His dark brows furrow at my words. "Why aren't ye good?"

I shrug. "I don't know. I thought the degree I studied would let me help people, and then I find out I'm more messed up than some of my clients would be. How am I meant to help others when I don't even know how to fix myself?"

Even I can hear the woeful tone in my voice. When I walked off the stage with my degree in hand, I thought life was perfect. I believed it. I just don't know if I do anymore.

"One thing I did learn from Ma is that ye can't allow others to define ye. Ye're the only person who can decide what ye want to be. If you want to be like yer folks, then so be it. But ye have that choice. Not them. Not me. Nobody else."

I can't help but smile. "You know, for a biker you're quite philosophical."

Monster chuckles and shakes his head. "It's Ma. She taught me all these things. At the time, I was convinced she was going crazy. But now, I realise she was right all along. I chose to run the club in my own way. I could have taken after my Da, but I vowed not to. And I don't. Not now, not ever. And I will never be like he was."

I nod slowly, understanding dawning on me. 'Thank you."

"Fer what?" he asks me.

I shake my head and turn away from his dark gaze. I don't know what to say. *Thank you for saving me, for keeping me safe, for making me feel. For showing me that I can be a good person.* Not one of those can encapsulate what I'm feeling right now. So, I opt for a simple answer. "For being you."

"There's nobody else to be," he tells me. "For a long time, I didn't want to admit that when I enjoyed killin'. But someone pointed out it was the *who* not the *what*. We work with a few detectives at Scotland Yard who give us names, and we finish the jobs they can't."

"What do you mean? Surely that's illegal. Being a vigilante doesn't make it right."

Monster turns to me and pierces me with his dark stare. "We've taken the lives of men who do very bad things. There's a lot of evil in the world. With Tye's skills, we're able to find them before law enforcement."

"And now they're all dead."

"Aye," he confirms. "Because they feckin' deserved it. When we go to their hideouts, we find the women and children they've taken, kept prisoner."

A cold shiver trickles down my spine at his words. Those are horror stories you read about, or hear about on television, not learn about in real life.

"Then why do they call you Monster?" I ask genuinely curious. "I mean, you don't scare me. And it sounds like you do a lot of good. It doesn't make sense."

This causes him to chuckle. "When I was younger, I was a handful. When Da told me not to do somethin', I'd go out and do it." He gets a faraway look in his eyes then.

"Aye, ye were a cheeky wee bastard," Rebel cuts in. "Fecker almost took my eye out when we were out on the piss one night." He laughs when he tells the story. "I was two sheets to the wind when Monster here walked into the pub. I'd started early that day," he recollects. "Lost me job, was feckin' pissed about it. Probably had ten pints in me by the time this arsehole walks in."

"Aye, you'd been hitting on a poor girl who was out with her mates," Monster throws back. "I was savin' ye from yerself," he tells Rebel. "Fuckin' pain in my arse."

"Takes one to know one," the VP retorts, and both men laugh.

There's a deep friendship between these men. I'd love to dip in more to their connection, to find out what makes them tick. To listen to their lives and offer advice, solace. I now see them as family, rather than strangers. But once all this is over with my mum and Patrick, I'm going to have to leave. The realisation dawns on me, and for a moment, my chest aches.

"Friendship turned family after that," Cathal says. "Ma always called me her wee monster. It was a name I had lived up to. Raisin' a youngen who was stubborn wasn't easy for her. I was a feckin' monster, but she loved me anyway."

I can't help but smile at that. "So the name stuck?"

"Aye, I quite like it. Not that I think of myself as bad," he says with a shrug. "But it's how other people see me. I don't give a shite what someone says about me. I've always lived my life like that."

"Life's too fuckin' short to care," Rebel says. "If you live day in and day out worried about what some other bastard thinks of ye, you'll never be happy." His words sink in. "They call me a feckin' Rebel. I'm proud of it. I don't follow the rules. I colour outside the lines," he tells me. "I love my life."

Except for the fact that you're in love with Callia and haven't told her. I keep my thought to myself. I don't want to get involved. I just hate seeing the girl fawn over him when he clearly isn't ready to make a move. Maybe one day.

Everyone falls silent as we lie there in the dimly lit hangar. It's silent when there aren't any planes coming in. I use the quiet to calm my mind and breathe deeply. My eyes are closed as I lie there. A spark shoots through me when I feel Monster's fingers reach for mine. It's a gentle reassurance of his presence. I tangle my fingers with his. Even though we don't say a word, it eases the ache in my chest. I force any emotion from my mind, from my heart, because this is going to be over soon, and I'm going to have to walk away from him.

We can't be together. There's no way this will work, because we each have different lives. Our paths may have crossed for this short time, but that's all it was. Nothing more. And I can't allow myself to feel anything; I need to focus on moving on. Instead of thinking about him, I think about my mum.

With every passing minute, and hour, the closer we get to the moment of retribution. Soon, we'll see my mother as she returns to London. I don't know what to expect, but whatever is coming, I have to be ready.

CHAPTER TWENTY

Monster

"Monster," Rebel's deep voice wakes me suddenly.

I didn't think we'd ever get here, but as I push to my feet, I see the men rushing around. She's coming. I glance around and find Miren staring at nothing. I want to ask her if she's okay, but I'm still fighting my wants and desires.

"Is it time?" she asks instead, and I nod. "Okay."

The girl who's been so fuckin' cheeky for so long, who's fired me up more than anyone ever has, looks fragile. She looks as if she's now broken.

"It's goin' ta all work out," I tell her, but when she looks at me, when those usually sparkling eyes land on mine, I see the dull stormy grey that makes my chest ache.

I can't fight this. I've tried. I want her. There's no more denyin' myself something good, something beautiful. I make a choice and go to her. Stopping right in front of her, I cup her face in my hands and hold her steady.

"I can't do this," she tells me in a pained whisper that seeps right through my hardened shell.

I nod. "Aye, ye can do anythin' ye want," I tell her confidently. "Where's the girl who walked into my club and told me to stop being rude to her? That fire I saw in ye needs to come out now. Because I can't lose ye."

Her eyes widen in surprise. Shock is painted all over her face. If I had to be honest, I'm just as shocked. I didn't expect to say those words to her. I didn't even think about them before they came out of my mouth.

"It's going to be okay." My voice is filled with confidence, because I know no matter what happens, she'll be safe.

"Monster, the plane is landing." Rebel's voice is tinged in excited energy.

The fecker loves to torture, he enjoys being out

on a job. I can't imagine what is runnin' through his mind. There's a chair with thick leather cuffs ready for Sinéad. She'll be questioned here. I wanted to take her back to Belfast, but it's too much hassle.

We have contacts in London who can do a clean-up if need be. And I'm pretty sure, they'll be needed. I take Miren's hand and lead her to where Rebel and Racer are hidden. We can't attack before she's disembarked, so we wait.

The moment it happens, we move. Miren is right behind me, and the men already have Sinéad in their clutches when she sees us. Her two guards are apprehended before they can draw their weapons.

"Miren?" Sinéad's voice is filled with shock. She turns her glare on me, then Rebel, and finally Racer before she looks back at her daughter. I wonder if she's about to beg for her life. "What have you done?"

"I have to say," I start with a smirk. "I'm impressed at the way you're able to change the accent. A Belfast accent doesn't truly ever go away. Does it Sinéad? Or do I call you Mrs Bragan?" I release Miren for a moment and make my way to her mother.

"I don't know what you're—"

"I think yer daughter wants to have a word," I tell her with a smile.

Stepping aside, I look at Miren who's trembling. She's nervous. Her hands are twisted as she regards the woman who raised her. I can't imagine how it must feel to come face-to-face with yer mother knowing she lied to you yer whole life.

"Why did you lie? Why didn't you tell me who you really were?" Her whispers are loud enough that we can all hear them, and the pain in her voice is evident.

My chest once again tightens. All this back and forth between Miren and me has taken a toll on my feelin's for her. I've fought it, I've given in, and I've raged with myself. But it's still her I want. There's no doubt about it. She's going to do great things in her life, and I want to be right by her side. It's stupid to even think this shite while she's waiting on her ma to respond.

"What did this man say to you? Miren, you must listen to me," Sinéad pleads, her gaze locked on her daughter, but I can tell from the way she's blinking she's also taking in her surroundings.

A woman like her will be looking for a way out of this. She'll most certainly be wanting to escape, to free herself and get far away.

But that's not happening.

"Why do you keep lying to me?!" Miren's voice booms now, louder than I've ever heard her. She moves swiftly, stopping inches from her mother. "Tell me the fucking truth," she orders confidently.

The girl who was earlier trembling is gone and in her place is a feckin' warrior. I've never been so attracted to her as I am right now. Seein' her strength makes me want to bring it out of her more and more.

"I had to protect you," Sinéad whispers. "You were the only thing I ever needed. The organisation was my father's. Your grandfather wouldn't listen to reason. Even though I never wanted it, he forced me to step up once he died."

"And Monster? His family? What about his father and mother?" She flicks her gaze to me, and Sinéad follows suit. "You killed them. You're the monster, not him."

"They needed to pay for their sins. His father was going to kill me!" Sinéad's outburst has my blood steaming in my veins.

I want to end her now, but we still have more to ask. There are so many questions, and I need answers before she pays for what she's done.

Suddenly, Miren moves. Her hand swipes up, and it's only when crimson spurts from her mother's arm that I realise she's carrying a knife. I race forward and grab Miren. "What the feck are ye doin', wee fox?"

"I just wanted to see if she bleeds," Miren speaks. The words come out as if she's in a trance. "You hurt innocent people," she tells her ma. "And you have to pay for those sins. I no longer know you. I never have. I'm not your daughter. And if you survive this, I don't want to ever hear from you, or hear of you, again."

Miren breaks down, falling into my arms, and I gesture with my head for the men to take Sinéad into the hangar. The screaming from her mother has Miren shaking in my arms. I take the knife from her hand and push it into my pocket. There's blood all over her arm and hands. Thankfully, she's not hurt.

"Don't ye ever do that again," I admonish the girl. Woman. She's a feckin' woman. Sometimes, she's so delicate I think of her as forbidden fruit, but in the same breath, I want to spank her arse.

"She needed to feel some form of pain. I wanted her to feel something for me." Miren looks up as tears stream from her face. "I wanted her to look at me with emotion, but all I saw was a dead stare. There's nothing inside her, Cathal."

I want nothin' more than to save Miren. To hide her from the ugliness in the world. But it wouldn't make her stronger; it would hinder her. Just like Sinéad did to her. What the woman did to her daughter wasn't out of love. It didn't ensure she was an independent woman who could handle things. She lied to *keep her safe*, but in the end, she created a broken-hearted girl.

"You will come out of this better for it," I tell her. "Yer ma, on the other hand, she's not going to walk away from this. Will you wait with Racer while I talk to her?"

"Yeah."

I leave her, even though I don't want to. But she doesn't need to see this. I find Rebel watching Sinéad closely.

Racer glances up when I enter and I tell him, "Watch Miren." I trust him, and I know he'll ensure she's safe. Then my focus is on the woman bound to the chair. "We finally meet," I say as I stop in front of her. Pulling the knife from my pocket, I look it over. "Seems like yer wee girl is good with a blade."

"You, let her go," she orders me, causing me to chuckle. She's in no feckin' position to tell me what to do. "She's not to be harmed in any way. Are you listening to me? My men will find you, and when they do, you'll be sorry you breathed the same air as her."

Anger surges through me. Without thinking, I tangle my fingers in her long red hair and fist the locks, pulling her head back so she's looking directly at me.

"Ye're not a mother. Ye left her to fend for herself with Patrick. Do ye know what the fucker did to her? And now ye want to come in here and order me around? I'm goin' ta to make Miren cry, and scream, and she's goin' ta feckin' claw at my skin. And ye know how I'm goin' ta do that? When I fuck her, over and over again. Because she wants me to."

Sinéad spits in my face. It hits my cheek. "Ye feckin' touch her, and I'll have ye killed. You'll be feckin' tortured before ye take yer final feckin' breath!" The deep, familiar accent returns in her angry retort.

"There it is. There's the real Sinéad Bragan."

Offering her a smile, I rise to full height before swiping the saliva from my cheek. Then I press the blade to hers. A worthy mother would have taken her daughter out of love, not out of fear of losing her fuckin' organisation.

"Where is Patrick?" I ask, even though I'm sure she won't tell me. I know for a fact she knows where he is because he's the one she's been hidin' from. The woman isn't stupid.

"Gone."

"Where?"

She looks up at me as I press the blade into her face. I'm not afraid of makin' someone talk, especially if the person deserves it. The crimson drips over my fingers and the blade, but I don't let up. I'll happily bleed her out right here. It's the first time I've ever hurt a woman. Doesn't matter who she is, but I know it will be the last time.

For the first time in my life, I'm livin' up to the dark side of the nickname Ma gave me.

"You don't realise it. You're too fuckin' focused on yer plan for revenge to see the bigger picture here, Monster," she tells me, but I'm still not sure what the feck she's talkin' about. "

"What bigger picture? My folks are dead because of ye."

"It's not about you, and it's not about your folks. It's about the Royal Bastards. He won't hurt Miren, and if she's with you, you're probably safe. But I'll tell you somethin' for nothin'—those girls at your club, watch out because a snake is beautiful to some and lethal to others," Sinéad tells me before an explosion is set off outside, and I forget about the woman before me and rush out to the one who's stolen my feckin' heart.

The two guards who arrived with Sinéad are dead. My two men are on the ground, but they're alive. The explosion was from the small plane Sinéad arrived in. Thankfully, Miren was beside the hangar when it went off.

Racer nears me, with Miren following close behind. "What the feck happened?" I ask.

My boyo shrugs. "Don't know. One of the guards had a phone ringin' incessantly. We moved away from him because it was annoyin' us, and then suddenly, there's a feckin' explosion in the front of the plane. I didn't see anyone inside, and nobody walked out, so it must have been done before her flight took off."

We head back into the hangar. I'm tense, my shoulders are hunched, and my hands are fisted. The need for violence is coursin' through me. I want to kill someone. The woman who's bound to the chair in front of me is the only person who can give me answers. The bomb would have killed her if they were still in the air. She must have known about it.

Sinéad stares at me before she smiles as I near her, and she says, "I would recommend you go home because the shite is about to hit the fan."

Miren gasps at her mother's accent. It's probably the first time she's ever heard it. "How...?"

Sinéad looks at her daughter. "I had such high hopes for you," she tells her. Sirens in the distance alert me that we need to go. When we planned our trip to intercept Sinéad, I called our contact at Scotland Yard.

No doubt MI5 will be on their way too. "Your father would have killed you the moment you were born had he known about the will. But now it's done. You're free. I did all this for you."

"Free from what?" Miren asks as confusion creases her brow.

"An heir to a throne is only in line if another isn't stepping up to take the lead." Her words make no sense. Miren is her only daughter. There's no son, we looked into both Sinéad and Patrick.

"I should kill ye fer spoutin' yer shite," I tell her as I look down at the woman who destroyed my life. "But rottin' in prison is just as grand. Ye'll never get out. Life in there will ensure ye pay, day in and day out. And as you get older, and the shitehole you're goin' ta makes you want to kill yerself, I hope you can't. I hope that you live to yer last breath, and the guilt eats away at ye until you can't think straight."

"Miren," she calls, ignoring me. But the flinch I noticed on her face as I spoke confirms she heard every word. "I hope that your life is free and happy now. You'll thank me when you learn the truth. I did it all for you. Patrick will never come for you again."

"Who is he going after?" Miren is in her mother's face, leaning in as they glare at each other. "Tell me."

"You'll see."

"Lies right up until the end. Goodbye," Miren tells her as the cars pull up.

I'm sure they've brought the whole feckin' force as they rush into the hangar. Jones, our contact at the Yard, offers me a nod, and I take Miren, and we leave. I still need to find Patrick.

But for now, it's time to go home.

CHAPTER TWENTY ONE

Miren

When the plane lands, Monster's phone starts beeping wildly. He pulls it from his pocket and taps at the screen. Rebel, Racer, and I walk on, but Monster stops, and it's only when he doesn't reply to Rebel do we notice he's behind us.

"Fuck," he curses as he looks up at us. "That's why Sinéad flew back to London. She knew we'd come to intercept her flight. It was all a set-up."

His fingers tighten around his phone until his knuckles turn white. I'm sure he's about to snap the phone in half.

"What are you talking about, boyo?" Rebel questions, as confused as the rest of us.

"Patrick tried to get into the compound. He's in Belfast. And he's after the club."

There's no time to delay. We make our way out of the airport to find Sully waiting. A breath of relief escapes my lips when I see him. I don't know if the others are safe, but so far, all we can do is hope.

The moment we're in the van, Sully takes off. "There was an attack on the clubhouse. Everyone is alive, but the place is a mess. I think there's more to it than just Patrick trying his luck on our home, though."

"What makes you say that?" Monster questions.

He's in the front seat beside Sully, while Rebel, Racer, and I are in the back, listening to the conversation.

"He left a note. It's so fuckin' cliché, but he said he wants the girl."

"Me?" I squeak, surprised.

I know my father would need me if he wanted to take over the organisation, but he'll need me dead. And I don't want to die.

"No, actually," Sully says, glancing in the rear view mirror. "He wants Calli," he informs us, but that makes even less sense.

The more I try to work out what she could mean to Patrick, I can't come up with a solution. She's never mentioned him before, not even when the men were looking for him. When Tye spoke about having to investigate Bragan, it was no secret who the Royal Bastards were after.

"Did he say why?" Rebel asks, his tone flat, uncaring, but his eyes tell a different story.

Even though he's not looking at me, I'm pretty sure he's burning a hole through the back of my head.

"No reason. He just said we need to have her go to him before seven tomorrow morning. Once he has her, he'll leave us be."

"She can't go," I pipe up. I haven't known her for that long, but she's become a friend to me. She was one of the first people to accept me into the club, into the family. "Monster?"

"Aye," he says. "Miren is right. We need to bring Patrick closer, lure him into a false sense of security, and then we can bring him down. With Sinéad and him out of the picture, perhaps we can finally stop lookin' over our shoulders."

My stomach twists with anxiety when I think about all the heartache my family have brought on these people. And now one of my best friends is being targeted by my father. I never knew I could be capable of hate, but right now I do hate him.

We pull into the grounds of the clubhouse, and I'm out of the van before I can rethink my actions. I race into the house and up the stairs. I don't find Callia in her room. Panic sets in. I hope she hasn't gone to him already. Maybe she went to see him and ask him to reconsider.

No.

She couldn't have.

When I reach my bedroom, I find Lia on my bed, and I sigh with relief. "Fuck," I curse. "I thought you went to him."

She races into my arms, and her long blonde hair gets tangled in my fingers as I hold her close. But then, she suddenly says, "I couldn't leave without saying goodbye."

I pull away and look at her. My hands holding onto her upper arms. "What? No. You can't go with him. He's the fucking devil. He's going to kill you."

"No," she says while shaking her head. "He's not going to hurt me. I don't know what he wants from me, but he's not going to kill me." Her words are confident, as if her explanation makes sense. It doesn't.

"What do you mean? You don't know what he's

capable of, but I do. I was in that house. He didn't care about me. He hurt me without a second thought, Lia." My pleas fall from my lips, but there's a look in her eyes that tells me she's not going to listen. She's made up her mind. "There has to be another way."

"There isn't, but I need you to do a couple of things for me, Miren." She pulls me to my bed, and we sit, side by side. "Please, promise me."

"Of course." I nod, but the moment I can, I'm going to tell Monster what she's planning. He must be able to stop her. Or Rebel. He can't just stand back and watch her go.

"You can't tell Monster about this. You can't even tell any of the girls. But Patrick has proof I'm his daughter."

My stomach bottoms out. My heart leaps into my throat, and my pulse thrums in my ears. I am deafened by the sound. My blank stare, which pins Lia to the spot, has her blinking as the tears fall down her cheeks.

"I saw the tests. I'm his biological daughter. And he needs me. I can't walk away from this. The only way to keep the club and the girls here safe is if I go with him."

I still can't find the words to respond. Shock has overtaken me. The whole day has been nothing more than a movie reel. Everything has been made up. This can't be real life.

"Let's find another way," I implore her, holding her hands in mine.

"The other thing I need you to do is be happy. Please. You and Monster are beautiful together. I need you both to just love each other. As much as you can."

This makes me laugh. It's a sad chuckle, pained. "I can't do this without you. Please, let the guys come up with a plan. They had one in the van on the way back from the airport. We can fix this." I look into those eyes that have only ever offered me kindness. Her smile is sad, and my heart aches.

"And the last thing I need from you is to give this to Rebel." She hands me a letter, which has my heart sinking.

On the front of the envelope is his name in her elegant scrawl. I can smell the sweet orange blossom perfume she wears all over it. A smile tilts my lips, and then I blink away the tears that are burning my eyes.

"You can't—"

"I've made up my mind, Miren. I've been through so much worse in my life. This is going to be fine. I know it is. I must do it for the family who showed me how to love again." She rises and pulls me into a hug. Then she's gone.

I grip the envelope in my hand and race from my room. I can't wait. If she's so convinced she's leaving, I need to get to Monster now. The doors to the room they have church in are closed, which means they're probably in a meeting, and I shouldn't disturb them, but I have to. This is Callia.

I race to the doors and shove them open to find all the men seated around the table. "Callia is gone," I tell them. "She came to my room to say goodbye, and then she told me she's going to Patrick. She said he's her father. I don't know how, but he's convinced her the only way to keep us safe is for her to go with him. She wanted you to have this," I tell Rebel and hand him the envelope.

He pushes by me without a second glance. I know he's going to look for her, but I also know he won't find her. The rest of the men are on their feet, and they're out the door once Monster shouts for them to find her.

He stops in front of me and pulls me into the room. "Tell me everything she said. I want to know it all. And then we'll find Lia and kill Patrick."

I follow him inside and sit. It's time for more truths. This time, they're not mine, but Callia's.

Two Days Later

We've looked everywhere. It's as if she's disappeared into nothing. Tye rushes into the lounge, his laptop perched on his arm as he holds onto it. "I've found them. I think. They're in Dublin. Patrick had a meeting with a few of his contacts down there. It seems he wanted passage out of Ireland without being seen. Not sure why he went to them, but—"

"I'll call Razor. He's one of the nomads I met while I was on my travels," Sully says. He's on his feet, his phone in hand as he makes the call. I look to Monster who's on his phone. I feel helpless. I can't do anything. Convinced that if they were to go South, I'd have to stay here. Monster has kept me in the house for the past couple of days. I can't go out into the garden, and he most certainly won't let me try to call Callia.

Rebel walks into the room and flicks on the telly where the breaking news has just hit.

"Today, in a shocking discovery, Scotland Yard and MI5 have confirmed the arrest of Sinéad Bragan. She's been taken into custody where she will stand trial for a myriad of murders and her connection with the Irish mob. For ten years, they've been searching for her, but a breakthrough came when a source tipped off the peelers as to her whereabouts. She'd changed her appearance and was living in hiding, where she told law enforcement she feared for her life. It turns out, she had tried pinning her crimes on her husband, notorious criminal, Patrick Bragan. If you know the whereabouts of this man, please contact local authorities immediately."

"Now we know why he needed to get out of here so quickly," Monster says as Sully returns.

"Aye, when I questioned Sinéad, she said somethin' about another heir," Monster says. "It didn't make sense until now. Callia is the daughter Patrick didn't know about."

"But who the fuck is her mother?" Rebel bites out in frustration. "She lived in a foster home most of her young life. When I found her, she was a runaway," he says.

I'm shocked that she never mentioned this to me. There were times I could see fear in her eyes when she spoke of her past, but she didn't tell me she was in foster care, she merely said her folks weren't the nicest people.

"Aye," Monster agrees. "A runaway who needed a place to hide. But what if she weren't hidin' from her foster folks? What if she was hidin' from Patrick all these years?"

Realisation dawns on me then. All this time I was befriending my half-sister, and I didn't know it. It's my fault she's gone. "And I brought him back here."

"Nothin' is on you," Monster says as he pulls me into his arms. "Get Tye on the computer. Let's find these bastards." He leaves the room with me in tow after giving the order. In his bedroom, he sits me down on the bed and drops to a crouch in front of me. "This isn't on you. Do you understand me?"

I nod, but I can't find the words. "I should go." I look up and stare at him. "I can't stay here when I brought the devil to your home."

"You belong here," he tells me firmly. "You're not leaving. We will find her. But you're mine. If ye haven't realised that yet, I'll make sure ye know just how much you're wanted here."

"But—"

My argument is cut short when Monster lifts me over his shoulder and make his way to the bathroom. He sets me down on the counter and turns on the shower. I watch him undress, still in awe at how beautiful he is.

"What are you doing?" I whisper when he starts taking off my shoes.

He doesn't respond, he merely helps me out of my

clothes. He's gentle, affectionate, placing kisses on my neck, shoulder, and then captures a nipple in his mouth.

When he finally has me completely naked, he leads me under the spray. "I'm makin' sure you're relaxed. There's a lot goin' on, but you must know that this is yer family now."

He drops to his knees before me and lifts my leg over his shoulder. I claw at the tiles when his tongue laps at my entrance. The water may be drenching us, but my arousal coats his tongue, causing him to groan as he looks up at me. A strong, alpha male who's devouring me as if I were his last meal.

The tightness in my shoulders eases somewhat, and I close my eyes to lose myself in the sensations. It's been a fucking horrible day, and yet Cathal makes sure I come with his fingers inside me and his tongue teasing my clit. Slowly, he rises again and looks down at me before gripping my arse and lifting me against him.

We fit.

We always fit.

His cock is hard and throbbing as he enters me.

"So fucking good," Cathal murmurs as he thrusts.

He's fully seated inside me. His body fitting against

mine, inside mine, perfectly. My hands tangle around his neck as my head drops back and my lashes flutter.

"Tell me you're mine," he orders in a deep growl. "Tell me, wee fox," he whispers along my lips.

I lift my head to meet his stare. My focus on those dark eyes that always hold me hostage, forcing me to feel things I never thought I would want to for a man like him. But when I respond, it's brutally honest.

"I'm yours. I've always been yours."

His body moves with mine. his hips slant up, causing his cock to hit just the perfect spot, which has my toes curling in bliss.

It's fast, passionate. We're both needy, both broken and desperate to be healed by our connection. I want nothing more than to lose myself to him, and I let go. I forget the pain of the past few hours, and I allow Monster to shatter me open and fill my cracks with parts of him.

"Today you're coming on my cock, and I'm goin' ta fill that pretty little cunt with my seed," he tells me before reaching for my clit and circling it, pinching it harshly. The pain and pleasure of his ministrations crash through me, sending me over the edge once more, and he keeps his promise. He fills me with his release as we stand under the warm, prickling spray.

EPILOGUE

Miren

Living with the family I've come to love is different to the one I grew up with. It was only ever my mother and me, and at the time, it was enough. I had friends, I had acquaintances, but none of them fulfilled me like the Royal Bastards do. It wasn't an easy road to get to where we are. But if I had to choose to do it all again, I would in a heartbeat.

Since I started my own practice in the city, I see patients four times a week, and the other days, I help at the club. I can't stay away, but I don't tell anyone I go there in the hopes that Callia returns. I know there's no way it will happen unless she somehow escapes from Patrick's clutches, but I still hold out hope. The lights and energy of O'Hagans is a welcome distraction from the fear that my best friend is gone, that she could be dead, and we just don't know.

It's been weeks since that night, and I don't know how to focus on anything other than the search for her, which continues daily. Even though there are jobs the guys are busy with, I know Tye is completely focused on the search. Since he's able to get into any computer system, he's been tracking both Scotland Yard and MI5 activity, and he just recently hacked into the FBI database. But there's no sign of Callia or Patrick.

The sound of kids running around in the garden drags my thoughts away from her and the worry to the news I have for Monster. He doesn't know I've taken a test, and soon enough, I'll tell him he's going to be a father. It's something we've spoken about, but we didn't ever think it would happen so soon. Granted, we were being risky a few weeks ago, so the fact that I was late, and the test came back positive is no surprise to me.

But I know he's going to want to put a ring on my finger. And that's what's held me back from telling him. I didn't want him to feel as if he has to marry me. I know Cathal, though. He wants to do everything by the book. Part of it is how he was raised. His mother taught him to respect all women and to care for and nurture the woman he's with. And he does that in abundance.

"What are ye doing out here?" Rebel asks as he saunters up to the doorway.

Even though the kids we're watching for the day are out in the garden, it's cold. The temperature has dropped considerably over the past few days.

"Figured I'd get some fresh air," I tell him. When I first arrived, Rebel wasn't overly friendly. He greeted me, but I could tell he didn't trust me. To be fair to him, he was right. There were things I was hiding. "How are you doing?"

"Aye, I'm grand." His dark hair is wet from the drizzle, while his green eyes seem to shimmer when he smiles. They're like endless pools as they lock on mine. "I know I wasn't ye biggest fan when ye arrived," he tells me. "But you're good fer him."

"Thank you, Rebel." I don't know his real name, but using his road name seems to go down well. In fact, all the men prefer their road names. I can understand why. It's never easy to have to recall where you've come from if your past is littered with darkness.

"Just don't ye hurt him," he warns me. "Or you'll have all of us feckers to deal with."

He chuckles as he grips my shoulder and offers it a gently squeeze. And then he leaves me to my thoughts. The evening's festivities are going to go on all night, and I'm tired already. As we draw nearer to Christmas, which is in a couple of weeks, I'm looking forward to exchanging gifts and helping with cooking dinner.

The clubhouse is lit up with fairy lights and adorned with decorations, and there are two enormous trees in two corners of the living room. When you have a family as big as this, you must make sure there's enough space for all the presents.

"Miren," Sully calls to me from the hallway, and I follow to find him in the reception room. It's furnished with three large sofas and a heavy wooden coffee table. The Christmas tree takes up most of the room, and I'm pretty sure there are animals living in the branches they're so big. "What's happening? Have ye told him yet?" He's the only one I told about the baby. With Callia gone, I needed a friend. Lia's absence has been difficult to take. I miss her daily, but Patrick has gone deep into hiding with her. The fear she's dead is always on my mind, but as I try to stay positive, I have found myself talking to Sully every day. He has become one of my confidantes in the clubhouse.

Now I'm living with Monster, my old room is empty. It's as if there's a hole in my heart since Lia left. But I know the brothers have been searching, while Tye has been hacking into computers to try to find a link somewhere. Rebel has been different, cold, closed off. And I know he's worried.

"Not yet," I whisper. "He's on his way back now. He's had to go out with Rev this morning."

When Cathal told me he was heading to a service with Hadrian, I was surprised. He told me once he hadn't been to church since before his mother was killed. So for him to go today must have been important.

"He's goin' ta be shocked. I doubt he ever saw himself as a father, but I know he'll be a grand one," Sully tells me with a smile. He's like the big brother I never had but always wanted. There's safety in his arms as he pulls me into a bear hug. "The two of ye will make the most amazing parents. I know you will."

He has been supportive since I told him. He found me sitting in the living room near the fire one night a couple of weeks ago. I was lost in thought; my concern about telling Monster I'm pregnant was worrying me. Not because I didn't think he'd be happy, but it was unplanned. I knew Cathal was out with the boys, so I was able to ponder how to tell him. Sully offered me advice; he told me I should be honest and allow Monster to decide. He said that things will work out because he knew the man behind the cut and patch, and he'd love having a family. It was that night I realised if the question came up, I would say yes to marrying Cathal without a doubt.

"When is dinner? I'm feckin' starvin'," Racer complains as he walks into the room. He's one of the newest members who patched in at twenty-two. Even though he's my age, sometimes he comes across as much younger.

"Should be soon," I tell him with a smile. "I thought you'd just eaten?"

"Aye, but I could do with something more. Growin' boy and all." Racer laughs out loud as he rubs his flat stomach, causing us to laugh at his antics.

"Enough," Rebel growls as he pushes by Racer and Tye who are just entering the room. The distant sound of a door slamming confirms he's not happy. I know he's angry because we're laughing, and Callia is gone. I understand the reasoning behind his anger.

"Eejit, he needs to realise family are here to support him. We must try to stay positive in the darkest of times," Sully bites out. "I need to get to work." He turns back to me and gives me a quick kiss on the cheek. "Good luck," he tells me with a wink.

"Wee fox," Monster's nickname for me is murmured in his voice as he enters after Sully leaves. "What's going on here?" he asks when he sees everyone in the living room. A few guys are on the sofas, others at the tree, trying to pluck the ornaments from the needles.

"Not much," I tell him. "Rebel is in a bad mood, Racer is making his life hell, and Sully is offering me advice on something."

"Nothin' new then?" He kisses me, and I forget that everyone can see us.

It's only been a few hours without him, and yet it feels like weeks, months. Whenever we're apart, I miss him. There's an ache deep inside me that reminds me I'm his and he's mine. I still can't believe we're here, after the rough start we had.

"I need to talk to you. In private, please," I whisper in his ear, and he takes my hand without question and leads me up to our suite.

I love living in the clubhouse, and I am thankful we have our own wing, our own little apartment, but we're still within walking distance of our family.

Cathal turns to me the moment the door shuts and

pins me against it. His body heavy, commanding, as his voice rumbles, "What's wrong?"

The concern in his eyes makes my heart leap into my throat. The gentle way he cares for me is the complete opposite to how he looks. Tall, strong, brooding. He looks like the Monster he's named after, but he's far from it.

"Well," I say as I push him away and escape his prison. "There's something I wanted to make sure was final and confirmed before I told you. So, it's been a couple of weeks since I found out and even though I know—"

"For feck sake, wee fox," Monster grumbles. "What the feck is wrong?"

Spinning on my heel, I pin him with a glare while I curl my lips into a small smile, so he knows I'm joking.

Then the words fall from my mouth before I have time to stop them. "If you're going to talk to our baby like that, I don't know if I want you around him or her."

I never thought I'd see a man stumped. But he is. His mouth falls open for a long moment, and I'm pretty sure he's stopped breathing. Seconds tick by, and the only sound I can hear is the thrum of my pulse in my ears.

When he finally says something, it's only one word. "What?"

I want to giggle, but I refrain. "You heard me."

Cathal rushes to me and drops to his knees in front of me. His hands hold my stomach, even though I'm far from showing, and he lays his ear against me.

"I'm sorry wee one," he whispers softly. "But I'm a biker, and I'm goin' ta curse like a feckin' sailor. Best tell ye ma she'll need ta get used to it."

My heart pitter-patters against my ribs at the sweetness of the moment. The bedroom door flies open, and Rebel stops dead in his tracks when he sees the scene in front of him. His mouth drops open for a split second before he curses, "Shite."

"What the fuck do ye want?" Monster doesn't turn to look at his VP, and I'm aware that he's still holding onto my stomach.

My cheeks heat with a blush when Rebel looks at me and smiles.

"Good lord, would both of you stop cursing like that?" I tell them while shaking my head.

"I'm sorry for bursting in, just wanted to confirm the next shipment is coming in tonight. I wanted to make sure Racer and Sully will be going with me." Those olive-green eyes that remind me of a serpent's flick between us.

"Aye, that's right," Monster says. "Now feck off." Rebel disappears quickly and shuts the door behind him. The moment we're alone, Cathal looks up at me. "This is perfect. Our lives may not be perfect, and they certainly didn't start out that way, but this wee one will have everything he or she wants."

"I'm not spoiling her," I bite out.

The glint in Monster's eyes tells me he may enjoy having a daughter. He'll probably shoot every boy who tries to date her. And I'm pretty sure she'll have her dad wrapped around her finger.

"Her?" he questions, his dark brow arching as he regards me with a smile.

"I don't know." I shrug. It's a hunch, but this is all new to me, so I may be way off base. "Let's just call it intuition. I may be wrong. It could be a mini version of you."

"Ach, aye, now that could be grand too. We'll have to just keep tryin' if it's not." This time, he waggles his eyebrows, which in turn has me rolling my eyes.

"Of course you'll want to spend all the time trying," I tease him as I head for the bedroom.

He follows close behind, and I know that no matter what happens, our family is growing and there is an abundance of love between us. Our home is overflowing with people who we trust, and who offer their loyalty. Not because they're forced to, but because they want to.

And nothing can take that away from us.

They may try, but they'll have a biker army to fight.

Now all we need to do is find Callia.

BONUS SCENE

Rebel

Working closely with Tye has kept my mind busy. I didn't want to think about what would happen to Callia when I realised she was gone. Her choice to go with Bragan still doesn't make sense to me. The woman may not be mine, because I'm too much of a feckin' eejit to tell her how I feel, but it doesn't stop me worryin' about her.

It's been years since she came to live at the clubhouse, since she became part of the family I'd chosen for myself. And in all that time, she was the only one who could make me feel anything. It was a protective need that would rear its head the moment she was in danger. But it was also desire, the attraction that coursed through my veins when I was close to her.

"This is feckin' frustratin'," Tye bites out as he shoves the mouse away from him. The sleek black desk is scratched by the thick silver bracelet he always wears. This is getting to him as much as it's getting to me.

"You'll find something," I tell him, my hand on his shoulder offers a squeeze of reassurance.

The pressure is on us all, but Tye feels it more than others. He's the only one who can do what he's doing. While we can all kill, it takes a special person to be able to understand the coding he's reading.

"Your confidence in me is nice, but I can't feckin' find anythin'."

He's an expert at what he does, and I have no doubt that somethin' will spring up. Scrollin' through pages of data can't be easy, and getting into locked networks is a skill I wish I had. If I did, I could have helped him. But my expertise lies in other areas.

The club is a home where each of us offers something unique. The only thing we all have in common is the fact that we can kill a man without a second thought. In sayin' that, though, we don't hurt innocents. It's part of our charter, our rules. It doesn't matter what situation we find ourselves in, we make sure those who are caught in the crossfire are safe.

Tye moves back to the computer before picking up his mug and swallowing back the coffee that's now ice cold. I brought it to him a couple of hours ago. But he doesn't notice the temperature. I leave him for a while and head into the lounge. Monster and Sully are at the table going through emails Tye printed out hours ago.

It's pissing down outside. I want to go for a ride, a long, never-ending feckin' ride. But Monster will want me to stay indoors. It's best we go out in pairs. Especially with the threat of Patrick still hangin' over us.

I'm happy for him. He has Miren who brings him down to earth when he loses his head. She's good for him. When she first arrived, I was convinced she would hurt the fecker. But it seems the girl is a welcome addition to the family.

"Anythin'?" I ask as I join them.

Christmas is in a couple of days, and I'm not looking forward to celebrating when Callia isn't here. She should be with us.

"Not yet," Sully tells me. "But there's a thread I found interesting. Banking information that I'm pretty sure is encrypted. I was goin' ta take it over to Tye to investigate, but it sounded like he needed a moment."

I look at Sully and nod in agreement. I can't deny it. I am worried about Tye's mindset while doing this. If I could pull him off what he's doing and tell him to take it easy, I would. But then we'd be back at square one. And at this point, we can't afford to do that. "Aye, he's stressed. Angry that he can't find anything to help us."

Sully shakes his head. "Ach, it's not his fault."

"It's what I told him."

I pull out a stack of papers and start scanning them myself. There is so much to go through, and I know it's going to take longer than any of us expected. The thing is, when a member of the mob goes into hiding, it's not like a petty criminal. These bastards have connections everywhere. We just need to find the right one.

"If it were any of us trying to find answers and coming up short, it would bother us too. He's a goodun, I know he'll come up with something. He's good at what he does." I flick through the pages as I say this, my focus on the names in the emails.

"I have no doubt about it," Monster agrees. "What is this?"

He hands me one of the emails he's been reading, and I scan it for a moment. Confused, I hand it to

Sully to have a look at. Glancing back at Monster, I say, "Name rings a bell, but I can't think where I heard it before."

"I know a Savage from my time in the States," Sully announces, which has both Monster and I staring at him. "I think we may be lookin' in the wrong place."

"Guys, I think you need to see this," Tye calls from the entrance to the living room. The three of us turn to look at the boyo, and the expression on his face tells me this is going to be big.

Maybe we'll get an early Christmas gift after all.

THE END

Ready to spend Christmas with the Royal Bastards? Why not dive into Yule Tyed, where we delve deeper into our favorite hacker's life. Head to Amazon!
https://geni.us/YT-OneClick

Also coming in to the world in March 2023 is Lucky Clover! If you'd like to preorder before it's live, you can do so now!
https://books2read.com/LC-OneClick

ACKNOWLEDGMENTS

My first full length MC romance was an adventure. It's the first time I've written in British English, and also, the first time I've had to be mindful of slang words which I had to make sure fit the characters.

Thank you to my editor, Candice, who worked on polishing up the manuscript.

And a massive thank you to Sheena for proofing this for me. Your advice and notes were invaluable. I'm so happy to have you on my team.

So much love and thanks to the amazing _Hydrus for the exclusive poem which fit the story perfectly.

It's always a pleasure collaborating with you.

To my PA, Caroline, as always, thank you for being the adult and making sure I get shit done.

To my readers, the amazing ladies in my reader group, The Deviants, thank you for always being so incredible, and to my Captive Angels for pimping my ass out, you ladies ROCK!

To all the bloggers, bookstagrammers, and booktokers, I hope that as my first MC romance, I've done it justice and you enjoyed it. Thank you for always taking time out of your busy lives to help support and promote me. You are incredible.

Mad love,

Dani xo

ALSO BY DANI RENÉ

Head to my website here for a full list of my
incredible titles

www.danirene.com

ABOUT THE AUTHOR

Dani is a *USA Today* Bestselling Author of seductive and deviant romance.

Her books range from the dark to emotional, but every hero is alpha, and each heroine is strong-willed, bringing the men down to their knees.

She now lives in the UK, after moving from Cape Town, exploring cemeteries and old buildings while plotting her next book.

When she's not writing, she can be found binge-watching the latest TV series, or working on graphic design. She has a healthy addiction to reading, tattoos, coffee, and ice cream.

www.danirene.com | info@danirene.com

Find me at @danireneauthor on

Facebook | Instagram | Pinterest | TikTok | Spotify

Printed in Great Britain
by Amazon